E

The Story of an Orange Lodge

SALZWASSER
VERLAG

B. Wagtale

The Story of an Orange Lodge

Reprint of the original, first published in 1864.

1st Edition 2022 | ISBN: 978-3-75259-530-7

Verlag (Publisher): Salzwasser Verlag GmbH, Zeilweg 44, 60439 Frankfurt, Deutschland
Vertretungsberechtigt (Authorized to represent): E. Roepke, Zeilweg 44, 60439 Frankfurt, Deutschland
Druck (Print): Books on Demand GmbH, In de Tarpen 42, 22848 Norderstedt, Deutschland

THE STORY

OF

AN ORANGE LODGE,

&c. &c.

THE STORY

OF

AN ORANGE LODGE:

A Chronicle of Dublin.

DEDICATED TO THE ORANGEMEN OF IRELAND.

BY BROTHER WAGTALE.

DUBLIN

1864.

THE STORY OF AN ORANGE LODGE:

A Chronicle of Dublin.

CHAPTER I.

> "When civil dudgeon first grew high,
> And men fell out they knew not why;
> When hard words, jealousies, and fears,
> Set folks together by the ears,
> And made them fight like mad or drunk
> For Dame Religion as for punk."

SOME fifty years ago there resided in Thomas-street—then, as at present, one of the most important trading districts of Dublin—a worthy alderman, named Elliott, who, by industry and uprightness, had succeeded in realizing a considerable fortune. The establishment in which he had been so fortunate was a remarkable one; so much so, indeed, that few could pass through Thomas-street, populous as that thoroughfare was, without observing it. A colossal statue, of strange and unearthly aspect, the object at once of wonder and speculation to the beholder, decorated its front—a hideous, ungainly monster, whose sinister countenance seemed to scowl at you in fiendish triumph as you passed, while his head (when the wind blew) has been known to turn and look down the street, as if in search of a victim to mark him for his own. In one hand he brandished a gleaming scimitar, and in the other he held forth a golden goblet, of which, while apparently inviting you to partake, he evidently defied you to venture upon the dangerous experiment. The juvenile mind (rich in Arabian lore), while contemplating it in awe and wonder, used to associate it with some mighty genius or enchanter, who besought of you to swallow a pernicious draught, more potent in its effects than all the physics, philters, or elixirs that were ever compounded from the days of Galen down to those of our own Holloway. The intelligent observer, however, who was neither fanciful nor nervous, had no difficulty in discovering the true character of this remarkable personage; for the announcement on the board beneath explained that the premises over which he presided was "*the Original Twankay and Bohea Emporium*," when, by an easy process of reasoning, he arrived at the fact that, despite the incongruity of figure, feature, and costume, the object of his curiosity was a native of the Celestial Empire—a mandarin of the first magnitude at least; and that the vessel in his hand was a harmless cup of tea, with which he was about to refresh himself, with the implied admonition to the beholders to follow his example. The establishment, which in fact was known as "the Sign of the Mandarin," had attained a wide celebrity, and was so well appreciated by the public, that people flocked to it from all parts of the city, certain of obtaining there the best value for their money, in tea that was strong enough to burst the vessel it was brewed in, and coffee such as the houris of Paradise may be supposed to regale the faithful with. But, famous and remarkable as was the "Original Twankay and Bohea Emporium," David Elliott, the proprietor, or, as he was more generally known, Alderman Elliott, was far more so; for, apart from his civic honours, which alone rendered him famous, he was celebrated throughout the city for being what Daniel O'Connell used to designate "a rampant Orangeman." Not one of your tame, degenerate, smooth-faced "brethren" known to Dublin at the present day, who has none of the old fire within him at all, who keeps his principles quietly to himself, fearing to own them in public, and who, instead of displaying his colours like a true blue of the olden time, furtively sneaks away at night to join his brethren at their place of meeting, hiding his orange scarf in his pocket, and never producing it, nor venturing to crow out a single "No surrender," or "Croppy, lie down," until he finds himself secure within the shelter of "the Lodge." No; David Elliott was no such milk-and-water character as this; he was a genuine Orangeman of the old Tory school; a thorough-going no-surrender man; ever ready, regardless of time or place, to show his colours and declare his principles. Most characters like him, at the period, would not only have been unpopular with the mass of the people, but would have been hated intensely, for party feeling at the time raged fiercely, and sectarian animosity divided the people into hostile sections, hating each other with an intensity happily unknown to the present generation, and never, we trust, to be again revived. But, although regarded with dislike by the more ultra of the Roman Catholic party, David Elliott was greatly esteemed by Catholics in general, who bore with his principles, obnoxious as they were, for sake of the man; for the fact was that Elliott, although a Protestant and an Orangeman, was, unlike most of his associates, by no means a bigot. In moments of enthusiasm, when heated with party feeling, and carried away by the Orange mania, he appeared intolerant and bigoted; but once the fever had subsided, he stood forth what he really was, a reasonable, just, and amiable man, as ready to associate with or befriend a Catholic as one of his own communion: thus it was that, on public occasions, when joining conspicuously in party demonstrations, his offensive displays would be borne by the crowd, not only with patience, but good humour, provoking such a remark as "Go on, Alderman; have it your own way; nothing from you will anger us;" while the same conduct in another would meet with execration or personal violence.

Still, however, he was an enthusiastic Orangeman, whose parallel could only be found in our day amongst the hot-headed brethren of Ulster, and he *seemed* a bigot of a virulent stamp; and, although he was strongly tinctured with true liberality, should any one have attributed liberal principles to him, he would have resented the imputation as an unpardonable insult. He was not only true blue himself, but all belonging to him were so too. It was his boast that, within the memory of man, an encroachment of Popish blood into his family (for so he used to express himself) had not taken place. "My mother," he would say, "was a Leslie, and my grandmother an Armstrong"—these names, which were borne at the time by two prominent leaders of the Orangemen of Ulster, were supposed to typify the very intensity of Orangeism—"my great grandfather was one of the first who rallied round King William's banner when he landed in this country; my father and I fought side by side in '98, and here am I now ready to die whenever my king and country require. Popish blood, Sir, would not mingle with mine—no, Sir, I defy it." And the worthy alderman would strike the table with his fist, and look fiercely around, as if expecting and defying contradiction. His enthusiasm on this point partook largely of the ludicrous. In the height of his fervour he had caused his only child, when an infant, to be christened within sight of the River Boyne, and with water, too, from that historic river, the baby being at the same time decorated with all the imposing insignia of the order. The name conferred upon the embryo Orangeman was an imposing one, "William Nassau Gustavus Adolphus." What grandeur and proud associations were wound up in these euphonious names!—whole pages of history, rich in exultant triumphs, were unfolded at the mention of them. The father delighted to roll them from his tongue in presence of his friends; and his domestics were enjoined, under heavy pains and penalties, never, in referring to the child, to omit one of them. On his arriving at the age of seven years, he had him duly admitted into the Orange fraternity, and solemnly initiated into all the mysteries of the association, on which occasion it is a recorded fact, that, in a tiny glass of whiskey toddy, Master William Nassau Gustavus Adolphus drank "the glorious, pious, and immortal memory," and afterwards sang, with a tact that augured wondrous performances from him in future years, that inspiriting ditty, "the Boyne Water." These traits of inherent genius sank deep in the father's heart, who watched with doting fondness the dawning genius of the son, and with hopefulness and pride awaited the time when his tender bud of promise should expand into a full-grown orange lily. Having been left a widower at an early period of his married life, his whole heart and affections became centred in his little motherless babe. Oh! with what pride and rapture did he watch for each new development of that genius his parent's heart assured him his infant son possessed; and how eagerly did he look forward to the day when he should become a distinguished Orangeman, and, like himself, a regular attendant at "the Lodge," where he should occasionally take the chair, and, in speeches of thrilling eloquence, propose and pass resolutions breathing loyalty to the throne, and attachment to the Protestant religion, and prove himself every inch an Orangeman! How far these anticipations were realized we shall shortly have an opportunity of judging.

The Orange Lodge to which Alderman Elliott belonged was celebrated amongst the fraternity for its enthusiastic "loyalty." It was familiarly known to the initiated as the "GRAND LODGE OF THE PURPLE ARCH AND THE SCARLET BANNER;" and its meetings were held in the first floor back of a sort of half tavern, whole public house, in St. Andrew-street. At this apartment, which bore the imposing name of "the Lodge," we shall now briefly glance. Though dingy, and even dirty, and by no means elegantly furnished, it possessed many ornamental features that rendered the *coup d'œil* in the highest degree striking and imposing. The walls were decorated with more than a dozen pictures, all of them the veriest daubs, it is true, but, in the Orangemen's estimation, perfect *chef d'œuvres* of art, or, as they were fond of terming them, "grand historical paintings," most of them purporting to illustrate the career, and shed lustre on the memory of King William the Third, but in reality sadly burlesquing that really famous man. Over the chimney-piece his majesty was conspicuous in a scarlet coat and Spanish hat, astride a prancing charger, "crossing the Boyne water," while the very bullet which is said in the song to have "grazed his arm" (from the dimensions of it evidently a six hundred pounder), was seen glancing harmlessly by, and making direct for a devoted wheelbarrow in the rere. Opposite to this he was represented in gigantic proportions, leading on to the charge a body of Lilliputian cavalry, who, eager for carnage, flourish their swords around their heads; while, upon an eminence hard by, supposed to be the Hill of Dunmore, but close enough to allow

King William's horse to browse upon its slope, might be seen that ill-fated monarch, James the Second, in a stooping posture, and evidently in the very extremity of terror, having one hand resting upon his knee, and shading his eyes with the other, to enable him the better to observe, from his inglorious security, the issue of the contest.

In another picture King William might be seen on the battle-field, in the midst of his generals, pointing contemptuously to his vanquished kinsman, who is seen in the back-ground, running timorously from the field, and looking behind at the signal defeat of his army, like Lot's wife at the destruction of Sodom.

In addition to such like pictures as these, there were numerous busts and statuettes of his majesty scattered with tasteful negligence around the room, with various other emblems of deep and cunning import, all reflecting upon that eventful period preceding the downfall of the dynasty of the Stuarts. A large table, covered with orange serge, stood in the centre of the room, upon which was placed a punch jug of capacious dimensions, having on one side of it an effigy of King William; the nasal feature so amply developed as to serve for the handle. This vessel, on nights of meeting, was always kept charged to the brim with the reeking compound. Here used David Elliott and some thirty others of the brethren, night after night, to assemble, in order, as the phrase went, "to transact the business of the Lodge," but in reality to imbibe whiskey punch *ad infinitum*, and indulge in so-called "loyal" songs and toasts; to propose and pass aimless resolutions, whose only object was to serve as vehicles for indulging in vituperation of their Roman Catholic fellow-countrymen and the creed they professed. This, with abundant laudation of the Orange institution, and of their own splendid selves in particular, constituted the actual business of the brethren; for business, in its literal sense, they had none. Upon these convivial occasions Alderman Elliott frequently remained out to unseasonable hours, and, as faithful chroniclers we regret to have to record, rarely returned home perfectly sober. This occurred, it is true, in the jovial old times, as they were called, when drunkenness, or, to use a milder phrase, the habit of indulging in strong drinks to excess, was considered, if not a virtue, as affording evidence of a finished and gentlemanly education; when he who was so well-seasoned as to be able to dispose of his two dozen tumblers of whiskey punch, or his third bottle of port, and afterwards get safely and steadily home, was considered a fine, dashing fellow, while the unfortunate wight who could not swallow a fourth of the quantity without reeling home, and being placed in the "lock-up," was a sorry fellow, a drunkard, and a vagabond. It was true, also, that the whiskey punch patronized by the brethren was of unexceptionable quality, such as connoisseurs would say at the time "had not a headach in a hogshead of it." Viewing his conduct in connexion with all this, we must admit that custom was in his favour, though as moralists and historians we are obliged to condemn him. David Elliott, however, was not, in the true acceptation of the term, a drunkard. Thrown by habit and association amongst drinking companions, he was obliged when amongst them to conform to their customs, but was otherwise temperate in his habits; for, although he did indulge occasionally in drink, he despised it in his heart. Had he not in early life been left a widower, and been deprived of the companion of his youth, it is probable he would not have fallen so low as to deserve our strictures, for the best safeguard for man through this world of temptation and wickedness is the companionship of a pure and loving wife. Deprived thus of the object of his early affections, who had been his friend and mentor, he was led into evil company, and for a time allowed drink to usurp the place of reason. During his visits to the Lodge he was invariably attended by a faithful domestic of his, rejoicing in the patronymic of Roderick Cormick, or, as he was more generally called, "Rody." This person never failed to attend upon him on nights of meeting, ostensibly to supply him with his great coat, or on some other pretence, but really to see him safe home. In justice to the brethren, it must be owned they possessed the virtue of hospitality to a remarkable extent, for on those occasions they never failed to summon Roderick before them, and to present him with a flowing bumper of what old Brother Coates—a devoted Orangeman, of whom we shall have much to say hereafter—delighted in designating "King Billy's cordial," or "rale Protestant punch;" with such he was required to drink "the glorious, pious, and immortal memory," a demand with which Rody, although a steadfast Roman, never failed to comply. If he did not swallow the entire at a draught without winking—a task of some difficulty, as the liquid in question was usually administered to him scalding hot, and double-shotted, as it were, with alcohol—he was obliged to repeat the dose; and it is on record that his throat has been frequently left in anything but a sanitary condition, from his anxiety to afford the brethren complete satisfaction.

Dividing his time between the business of the "Original Twankay and Bohea Emporium" and that pertaining to the "Grand Lodge of the Purple Arch and the Scarlet Banner," David Elliott passed many years of his life. And now his son, William Nassau, for such for shortness he used now to be called, approached man's estate, and the time drew near when all the father's fond expectations should be realized, and his darling son, the heir to his lineage and fortune, should take his place a complete and well-seasoned Orangeman. But, alas for the perversity of our nature, and the instability of human calculations, William Nassau, though born and bred in "loyalty," and reared up, as it were, at the feet of Gamaliel, an Orangeman from his youth, had, from the time when mature reason first began to develope itself in him, shown the utmost apathy, if not aversion, to the "good old cause," for so the Orangemen used to term the principles they professed; it was as if the young man had been so overdosed with Orangeism in his youth, that he had imbibed a nausea for it in after years. For a long time the father would not believe in this unnatural indifference on the part of his son; nay, even when the fact became patent, and the young man openly declared his aversion to the cherished cause, he refused to believe in the reality, nor could he permit himself to entertain the thought that William Nassau Gustavus Adolphus could really be less enthusiastic than himself in the cause he so much revered. It must, he thought, be a delusion on the part of the young man; and consoling himself with that belief, and believing that his apparent dislike to Orangeism proceeded from some unaccountable hallucination, which his ripening judgment would dissipate and remove, he still looked forward hopefully to maturer years, when his mind should become more settled, and his opinions formed, to see him fulfil with cheerfulness all his cherished expectations. But time wore on, and William Nassau reached his full age, but only to become the more confirmed in his repugnance to the Orange system, which he had now determined never to identify himself with. Added to this, the young fellow was able to adduce arguments and reasons for the principles he had adopted, with which his father was entirely unable to cope. The cruel fact could now no longer be denied. William Nassau Gustavus Adolphus Elliott, the only-son and heir of Alderman Elliott the Orangeman, had backslided from the holy cause to which he had been consecrated in his cradle, and would not allow himself to be "sworn in;" and his poor father, in consequence, sustained such misery as only they who feel themselves disgraced by the commission of some great crime on the part of a near relation can realize or imagine. In other respects, however, young Elliott was all that could be desired in a youth of his age. He was moral, intelligent, studious, and industrious, and seemed to possess all the good qualities of his father, without his vices: withal he was a cônscientious and sincere Protestant, much more so, indeed, than the blind zealots who, at that period at least, constituted the Orange confederation, whose whole creed consisted in sowing discord amongst their countrymen, by hurling insult and defiance upon such of them as were of the Ròman Catholic communion, and bleating out continuously in their ears the party watchwords of "No surrender," or "Croppy, lie down."

"I don't know what to make of you, boy," said the father, on one occasion, when the son had given a calm but firm refusal to become an Orangeman; "there does not appear to be a spark of loyal blood in your veins, although you've come of a loyal stock. You'll prove a disgrace to your family, and for your mother's sake I regret it. She was a Rutledge, and all belonging to her was of the right sort; but you, you lukewarm, unmanly fellow, will bring disgrace both on her family and mine."

These were hard words for young Elliott to bear, and sorely did they burn into his heart; for, though conscious that truth and justice were on his side, it grieved him to hear his mother's name associated with princiciples and characters he despised; for he remembered her as the good angel who had tended him in his childhood with all a mother's care and fondness, who had first taught him to know and serve God, and to look to Him as the source of all good, and who had sown in his heart the seeds of the very principles which now guided him; he therefore well knew that her gentle, pious nature had no sympathies with Orangeism or its followers. But, sad and grievous as was young Elliott's defection from the Orange cause, there was another circumstance connected with him with which the father was not yet acquainted, which was fated yet more to rend his paternal bosom, and to exercise the most important influence on his life.

Hardly had young Elliott arrived at man's estate when he fell passionately in love with a young girl, some few years his junior. This was Miss Lonergan, daughter of a widow, who owned the drapery establishment known as the sign of the Distaff, in the same street in which he and his father resided. It is unnecessary for us to explain where or by what means the young people had become acquainted; let it suffice to say that, by some of those mysterious agencies by which youths and maidens in all ages have contrived to find each other out, and become plighted lovers, young Elliott had met his mistress, and was accepted; to use great Cæsar's pithy sentence, "he came, he saw, he conquered," or *was* conquered, if the reader will; for Kate Lonergan was as pretty a girl of seventeen as could be met with in the city of Dublin, in a day's walk, and that is saying a great deal. She was as dangerous a girl, in fact, as any nice young man of one or two-and-twenty, who thought a good deal of his own importance, and did not mean to throw himself away in a hurry, could possibly meet with, for she would assuredly ensnare him: she was so fresh and fair, and "looked so bewitchingly simple;" and as for "the glance of her eye," it was quite as effective as ever was that of the dangerous siren who dwelt in the romantic regions of Killarney, and is said by Thomas Moore to have committed such ravages on the hearts of her unsuspecting victims. It will therefore be seen that, although William Nassau had not become an Orangeman, he had been duly "sworn in;" his vows, however, were harmless ones, for they were never to cease to love the confiding girl who had given him her whole heart—a pure and precious treasure he richly prized. Now, this was not one of your plain, matter-of-fact love affairs which ordinarily takes place, where the young people meet, and court each other in a business-like way, with the sanction of their respective parents, who look on approvingly while the gentle doves bill and coo together regularly and methodically, and eventually enter into the holy state of matrimony with all the usual formalities. In cases like these the pathway to happiness is strewn with flowers, and all is joy and gladness; exulting parents—joyous, though weeping sisters (looking forward with anxious hearts for their turn to be led to the Hymeneal altar)—hysterical maiden aunts, with wedding presents, breathing inarticulate blessings, —bridesmaids—orange blossoms—congratulations, and kisses. But with our young lovers the case was very different indeed: *their* path was beset with thorns, and all seemed dark, dismal, and unpromising.

And thus it was:—Kate Lonergan was not only a Roman Catholic, but belonged to a family celebrated for the ultramontane tendencies of its members. Her uncle was a monk of the order of St. Dominick, whose whole life had been one continued warfare against Protestantism, and who, at the very time we treat of, was on a pilgrimage to Loretto, to beseech the Lady of that place to banish heresy from these realms. Her family included a bishop, a parish priest, two or three curates, and a whole host of Fathers Johns and Peters, and Sisters Theresas, Marthas, and Marias, all active in the service of their generation upon home or foreign missions, or qualifying themselves for canonization within convent walls. Her deceased father, it was said, had been an active leader of the Ribbon confederacy, and also belonged to several other fraternities, whose object was to put every Protestant in the British dominions to the sword, and confiscate their property to the good of the Roman Catholic Church. Rumour said that the Widow Lonergan herself was a zealot of no common order; but rumour is an untruthful gossip, the twin sister of falsehood, who delights in mischief, and is not to be relied upon. Certain it was, however, that the widow and her daughter were faithful members of their Church, and were under the spiritual guardianship of that renowned theologian, the Rev. Dr. Dominick O'Flynn, who looked upon all aliens to his communion as reprobate, and certain, should they die in their unbelief, to inherit a perpetuity of torment in that torrid region which it is the desire of all Christians to steer clear of. It was whispered, too, that Mrs. Lonergan, with a laudable solicitude for the welfare of her soul, was undergoing a species of voluntary martyrdom, having laid herself under an obligation to St. Veronica (believed to be a warm patron of the Church), not to put scissors to her hair for seven years, and to dine upon fish three days in each week for a like period, and many there were who commiserated her for the privations she had subjected herself to; but we would not have been amongst the number—for, if it were true that she had made such a vow, she was no great sufferer after all. As for her hair, it was so remarkably fine and luxuriant, it would have been quite a pity to have parted with any of it; and her partiality for salmon, turbot, and other light trifles of the kind, rendered her abstinence from meat anything but a privation. In fact, it would have been absurd to pity her, for she thrived and flourished, and was fresh and blooming withal.

And now how untoward seemed the prospects of the young lovers! On the one hand was a youth sprung from a race of ultra Tories, who despised Roman Catholics, and contemned and abhorred their belief,—on the other, a young girl, whose family was remarkable for its ascetic Romanism, and for its implacable hatred to Protestantism,—each of them obstinately in love with the other. The Widow Lonergan, it was well known, would never permit her daughter to wed a heretic; and as for Alderman Elliott, he would rather see his son a lifeless corpse than the husband of a Catholic. Such, alas! were the extreme opinions prevailing at the time amongst the two orders of Christians who peopled this fair country. It is refreshing, however, to be enabled to record that, although sectarian differences thus separated their families, the young people trusted each other with unfaltering faith, and loved with all the intensity of their fresh and ardent natures; for love, which was planted in our breasts by the Creator, will assert its sway, regardless of the logic of the sectary, or the ban of the bigot. Seeing the chasm that lay between them, they had thought at one time of braving all dangers, and crossing it, unmindful of the peril of the adventure; and, the better to enable them to carry out their arrangements for an elopement, had taken into their confidence Rody Cormick, who has been already referred to; but Rody, who under a rough and apparently dull exterior possessed an ample fund of sound, good sense, strenuously dissuaded them from repairing to Gretna Green; and, taking a cool, business-like view of affairs, assured them there was no necessity for such precipitancy, and that, if they waited patiently, all would come right in the end. They took his advice, unpalatable though it was, and contented themselves for the present with the consolations afforded by occasional secret interviews, and the frequent interchange of *billets-doux*, which Rody contrived to carry to and fro, to the intense gratification of the writers, and to his own decided profit, as the deposit of many a glittering piece of silver in his broad brown hands by the grateful lovers substantially testified. And thus days wore on; the young people looking forward hopefully to the blissful future, when all obstacles to their union should be removed, and never once giving way to despair.

Now, Thomas-street, wherein the lovers dwelt, is a wide and populous thoroughfare, quite different from your genteel, half-private street, where the occupants are in most cases intimate with each other's appearance. People might live in Thomas-street for years, and yet remain total strangers to each other. Such being the case, it will not surprise the reader when we add that the lovers not only carried on their wooing unknown to their parents, but that the latter were perfect strangers to each other. So little idea, indeed, had the young lady's mother of the actual state of affairs, that she had privately entered into a treaty with Dr. O'Flynn for the marriage of Catherine to a faithful son of the Church, and a protegé of his reverence—a meek young man, in a long coat of sombre hue, a white neckcloth free from starch, and a shovel hat, who used to glide from door to door with his eyes on mother earth, collecting funds in aid of the Cornwall Mission. Oh, how they counted without their host! the youthful Juliet did not spurn the overtures of the noble County Paris more heartily than Catherine would have shrunk from an alliance with the collector. But we shall leave the lovers for the present, and commence another chapter, in which circumstances most eventful to them have to be recorded.

CHAPTER II.

> "For aught that ever I could read,
> Could ever hear by tale or history,
> The course of true love never did run smooth:
> But either it was different in blood;
> Or else misgrafted in respect of years;
> Or else it stood upon the choice of friends;
> Or, if there were a sympathy in choice,
> War, death, or sickness did lay siege to it."

UPON one of those festive occasions when Alderman Elliott was in the habit of meeting his brethren, and giving utterance for the thousandth time to that loyalty to the British crown and constitution which no one ever questioned, a deputation from one of the provincial lodges waited upon them, in order, as the spokesman of the party expressed himself, "to confer upon some points of vital importance to the body at large." After discussing these weighty matters, and refreshing themselves meanwhile with abundant potations of "King Billy's cordial," for which the "Grand Lodge of the Purple Arch and the Scarlet Banner" was famed throughout Orangedom, and having disposed of the usual "loyal" toasts, and, in speeches of a brilliancy that only they who worship devoutly at the shrine of Bacchus ever succeed in approaching, declared their readiness to turn out at a moment's notice, and annihilate all who presumed to differ from them in considering the laws prevailing in this kingdom (which at the time were chiefly remarkable for their intolerant and penal character) the most just and benign that this or any country was ever blessed with, and that he who attempted to modify or improve them was a dangerous revolutionist, to be shunned by all true men, and but a visionary enthusiast, who would "gild refined gold, or paint the lily" — after, we say, enjoying themselves thus, the members of this distinguished Lodge, by way of complimenting their provincial brothers, and entertaining themselves at the same time, decided on adjourning to the Theatre, where an actress of great celebrity was just then delighting the citizens of Dublin with her histrionic powers. To the Theatre, accordingly, Alderman Elliott and his confreres repaired, and there, for the present, we shall leave them.

Now it happened that, on the very same evening on which the Orangemen had thus decided on patronizing the drama, young Elliott and his affianced bride, by way of consoling themselves for past privations, had concerted measures also for going to the Theatre, in order to enjoy the pathetic tragedy of "Romeo and Juliet," which was announced for the occasion; and when the curtain rose our young friends were found occupying prominent seats in the boxes, and looking as happy for the time as a newly-married couple during the first week of the honeymoon. That they were delighted with the performance need hardly be observed; so deeply, indeed, did they sympathize with the unhappy lovers whose fate was being worked out before them, and whose position was so much akin to their own, that Catherine, unable to restrain her feelings,

> "Dropped tears as fast as the Arabia tree
> Its medicinal gum;"

and we are obliged to add that it was only by constantly remonstrating with her, and pretending to smile at her folly, that William Nassau could restrain himself from following her example. When the gifted Thespians who had represented the two principal characters of the drama appeared alive and well before the curtain, after having duly committed suicide, the delight of our lovers was so intense that, in common with the rest of the audience, they stood up and heartily applauded, in accordance with immemorial custom. At this very moment it happened that Mr. Elliott, who, as the reader is aware, was also present, distinctly heard a familiar voice repeat several times the exclamation "Bravo," upon each occasion with renewed emphasis. He felt puzzled and bewildered, but, looking up from the pit, where he and his brethren had been enjoying themselves, he discovered the source from whence the sounds had issued; for there was his son, flourishing his hat enthusiastically around his head, with Kate by his side, waving triumphantly her white kerchief, in token of their unqualified approbation of the performance. Mr. Elliott was astounded. He had never imagined his son to have been a lady's man before; on the contrary, owing to his distaste for politics, and his refusal to become an Orangeman, he had set him down as a dull, spiritless, young fellow, who had not sufficient courage to look a woman straight in the face. For a moment he seemed to doubt the evidence of his senses, and uncertain as to whether his own son really stood before him, and, turning to one of the brethren, he involuntarily exclaimed, as he directed his attention to the young man, "Bless my heart and soul! is that my son William Nassau up there?"

"It's nobody else," replied the person addressed; "yes, and as pretty a girl beside him as one could well fancy: the young fellow has got a sweet tooth."

"Why, that's the handsome Miss Lonergan," remarked another; "her father left her a very good fortune, and lots of young fellows are aspiring to her, in consequence. I knew the father well, and a worthy, decent fellow he was, albeit he was a Papist, and I believe a sincere one."

"What! old Nick Lonergan, of Thomas-street?" asked Bob Coates, with horror depicted in his countenance.

"The very man," replied the other.

"Why, he was the greatest rascal that ever escaped a halter," returned Mr. Coates. "He was the prime leader of the Ribbonmen of Leinster—a dangerous, terrible character, who belonged to every disloyal confederacy that has ever distracted the country—the Terry Alts, the Whiteboys, the Molly Maguires, the Flagellators, the Scarifiers, and the Billy Welters. How he escaped the gallows I never could understand."

"Bless my soul, I'm surprised and astonished," said poor Alderman Elliott; "how could a son of mine become acquainted with the daughter of such a man?"

"Well, all I have to say," returned the former speaker, "is this, that I knew Nicholas Lonergan well, having had extensive business dealings with him; and that I always found him a scrupulously honourable man, straightforward and correct in his dealings. I would have trusted him to any amount; and, as for his connexion with the illegal societies Bob Coates alludes to, I'm persuaded he was too sensible and industrious a man, and too much attached to his family, to have mixed himself up with them at all."

"All deception, my dear fellow—all deception," rejoined Coates; "he acted as you state to gull and deceive you and the public; but in his heart; d'ye mind, now—in his heart he was as great a rascal as ever lived."

"Well, I only wish that all rascals would practise the same kind of deception," rejoined the former, laughing gaily; "if they would do so, the community would be much the gainer. Old Nicholas Lonergan died a wealthy man, and every penny he possessed was earned by honest industry; of that I'm sure."

Here another of the company, who had been scanning the young people attentively for some time, remarked that he had frequently met the alderman's son in company with the young lady in question.

A light now burst upon David Elliott's mind. Here, thought he, is the key to William Nassau's disloyal conduct. He has placed his affections upon this young woman, who has taken advantage of her opportunities to impose upon his weak, unformed mind, and to sap and undermine his principles; perhaps, too, to pervert him from his faith. But on this point further consideration obliged him to admit he had no grounds for apprehension; for he knew his son to be far more seriously attached to the religious principles he had been nurtured in than he himself was; for it was with Elliott as with most of his brother Orangemen, that, while zealously contending for the Bible as the sole code for the Christian's guidance, and while loudly proclaiming his Protestantism, he seldom or never studied the sacred book he so much affected to revere, while his outward observance of religion consisted in a few casual visits to the house of God in the course of the year.

"You had better look sharp, Brother Elliott," continued the Orangeman who had last spoken; "your son and that young girl look very like lovers. The fact is, I have met them so frequently of late in my neighbourhood, when they always appeared on such familiar terms, that I looked upon them as near relations."

"Heavens and earth!" exclaimed another, "what would become of you, Elliott, if your son married a Papist?"

All this was terrible news for the poor alderman, who groaned with anguish. All hopes of his son's reformation seemed now shattered for ever.

As for Brother Coates, the aspect of affairs rendered him for the time speechless; for in the attachment of the young people he saw the darling object of his hopes frustrated and destroyed, as we shall shortly take occasion to explain.

Rousing himself from the stupor which these astounding revelations had thrown him into, Mr. Elliott exclaimed with energy, "This must be put a stop to at once. I shall take care that this clandestine and unnatural courtship shall proceed no further. I'll—I'll"——in his anger and mortification he was unable to find language to express himself. Miserable man that he was, he felt as if his son had inflicted some indelible disgrace upon him.

"There's but one course to purshue," said old Robert Coates, who was not remarkable for the purity of his English, "you must write at once to the mother of this young famale, and acquaint her with the entire business. Tell her to call off her daughter at once, as you'll never consent to her marriage with your son; and as for the young man himself, forbid him, on pain of being cut off with a shilling, ever to spake to the girl, and lecture the lad sevarely." And feeling that he had decided the fate of the young people, and clenched matters skilfully, Brother Coates looked around for that applause which his tact and ability, as he considered, had fairly entitled him to.

"I'll follow your advice, and that instantly," exclaimed Elliott, who would have proceeded then to carry out his threat, had not the brethren, by way of composing his ruffled feelings, and at the same time ministering to their own enjoyment, induced him to accompany them to a neighbouring tavern, where, with the aid of plenteous draughts of "King Billy's cordial," they discussed the momentous matters that had thus come to their knowledge.

We have intimated that Mr. Coates was discomposed at the prospect of young Elliott's intermarriage with the daughter of old Nicholas Lonergan, and we now give the reason. Bob Coates had an only daughter, whom, in the depth of his paternal love, he believed to be endowed with every grace that has ever been vouchsafed to woman. With this conviction, he had determined to give his friend and kinsman the benefit of the treasure, by bestowing her upon his son, for whose "guide, philosopher, and friend," he had from an early age determined her. Young Elliott, besides being a handsome, amiable, gentlemanly young fellow, whom most young ladies would admire, was considered by people who knew the world, and kept a sharp eye upon the main point, a decidedly "good match;" and Mr. Coates wisely thought that, in securing him for a son-in-law, he was not only serving the young man, but was providing very comfortably for his daughter. It was only natural, therefore, that when he saw the prize all but wedded to an alien, and she, in his own words, "a rank Papist," he should feel by no means composed or tranquil; so strong, indeed, were his feelings on the subject, that he privately registered a vow in heaven to separate the lovers at whatever cost.

In accordance with the course he had suggested to

Mr. Elliott, the mother of the young girl, the Widow Lonergan, was duly apprised of the heinous conduct of her daughter; and on his further entreaty, Dr. O'Flynn, the spiritual director of the family, was further enlightened on the subject. The consequence was that Kate, "the daintiest Kate in Christendom," was threatened with the displeasure of her mother and of holy Mother Church if she associated longer with that arch heretic, young Elliott; and portentous hints of nunneries were thrown out occasionally in her presence, that were expected to produce the most salutary results. But Catherine heeded not these warnings; for so great is the waywardness of human nature (especially of the female portion of it), that the efforts thus made to wean her affections from her lover only strengthened her in her attachment to him. Nor did our young friend, William Nassau, come off scatheless; for he was admonished just as Mr. Coates had advised, and even threatened to be disinherited if he disobeyed his father's injunction never again to hold any intercourse with the obnoxious young lady. But the interdiction thus placed upon the lovers was fruitless; for they communicated with each other as they had previously done: their meetings, it is true, were not so frequent as formerly, but then the love-letters were more constantly interchanged. All this, by some mysterious agency, became known to old Bob Coates, who hopped and twittered about with nervous anxiety as he became possessed of each piece of intelligence, and displayed all the activity of a tom-tit in discovering the plans and secrets of the lovers, and endeavouring to thwart them in their purposes. As for Alderman Elliott, although most earnest in his determination to deter his son from continuing his acquaintanceship with Miss Lonergan, he was continually remonstrated with by Mr. Coates for not adopting more vigorous measures; and the poor man would have had no peace, had he not adopted the expedient of pacifying his tormentor by keeping him well primed with "rale Protestant punch," a liquor in which his soul delighted, and thus, as it were, bought the old fellow off.

CHAPTER III.

"There is a devil haunts thee in the shape of a fat old man—why dost thou converse with that trunk of humours; that bolting-hutch of beastliness . . . . . that reverend vice; that gray iniquity; that father ruffian; that vanity in years? wherein is he good, but to taste sack and drink it? wherein neat and cleanly, but to carve a capon and eat it? wherein cunning, but in craft? wherein crafty, but in villany? wherein villanous, but in all things? wherein good, but in nothing?"

During the state of affairs narrated in the concluding part of the last chapter, Mr. Coates paid an evening visit to his friend Alderman Elliott. The old gentleman was evidently much dissatisfied with the continued intimacy of the lovers, and the supposed apathy of his friend on the subject; for his bearing was cold and distant, and he only returned unsatisfactory monosyllables to the hearty greeting he received; the alderman, suspecting that a storm was impending, waited with resignation for the explosion. After some time Bob Coates, heaving a sigh, roused himself for the task before him, and thus gave vent to his feelings:—

"I tell you what it is, Brother Elliott, if things go on further as they have, we'll be obliged to expel you from the Lodge; you're becoming quite lukewarm, and losing all interest in the cause; one can see it with half an eye; were it otherwise, you would never permit such doings to be perpetrated under your very nose."

"My dear fellow, what can you mean?" asked Elliott, with alarm. But without heeding him Bob Coates continued—

"No later than yesterday William Nassau and that Popish young famale opposite were seen walking arm-and-arm together, and they looking sweeter than honey at each other. It's not to be borne, so it's not; and as one of the family I protest against it. If things continue thus, they'll get married in spite of you: and then it's an accessary before the fact you'll be"—and, chafing with anger and indignation, he sternly regarded his kinsman.

In vain the alderman declared that he not only gave no encouragement to the courtship complained of, but that he never omitted an opportunity of dissuading his son from continuing the intimacy with the young person alluded to; but Mr. Coates was not to be satisfied, and insisted that his friend was conniving at the affair.

"My dear Bob, I can do no more," returned Elliott at last. "I am tired lecturing William Nassau on the subject; but he's so obstinate and headstrong, there's no making an impression on him; and then he argues with me in his turn, and talks of marrying for love, and all that sort of thing."

"Stuff and nonsense!" growled Mr. Coates.

"Surely," continued the alderman, "it should satisfy you when *I* remain staunch to the cause: a man cannot be accountable for the misconduct of his son, can he?"

· "That's all very well," returned old Coates, growing dictatorial and dogmatic; "but I maintain that you are not staunch. If you were the rale true blue I always considered you, rather than allow William Nassau to ally himself with a Popish family, you'd marry him at once to some respectable young woman of his own persuasion. There's many a man of well-tried loyalty would be glad to marry his daughter off-hand to him."

This home thrust, so skilfully delivered, the old fellow hoped would bring his own daughter on the tapis, but he was doomed to disappointment.

"My dear fellow, have reason," returned the alderman, with some show of testiness. "William Nassau is now of full age and his own master, and it is quite impossible to deal with him as if he were a child, or the mere puppet in my hands that you seem to think he is. I cannot control him as if he were my slave, nor shall I attempt to do so."

"Why didn't you nip the affair in the bud?" continued Coates, carried away by his earnestness. "And why did you take matters so quiet and easy when you saw him and the young famale together in the Theatre the other night?"

"What would you have had me do?" asked Elliott.

"What would I have you to do, is it? Why, I'd have stopped the performance; I'd have called out the military; I'd have made a parliamentary business of it;

I'd—I'd—I'd have brought the matter before the Court of King's Bench! That's the right shop for justice."

"Pooh! my dear fellow, that's quite nonsensical, and don't suit me at all," returned the alderman, with a spirit and determination that rather astonished his companion.

Mr. Coates, now seeing that it would be dangerous to attempt to push matters further, entered at once upon the real object of his visit, to which what he had previously uttered was but the prelude.

"David, my dear friend, you must excuse my zeal," said the old fellow, in a pacified tone. "You know I have no desire to bear too hard upon you, and that it would grieve me to the heart to cause you uneasiness."

"I am sure of it, Bob," returned the alderman, quite mollified towards his kinsman.

"Well, then, David, altho' I know you are still true blue, I cannot avoid asking you to give me one proof of your unshaken loyalty: if you'll do so, you'll remove a dead weight from my heart, and complately remove all the misgivings that have disturbed me as to your unfaltering faith in the cause."

"To be sure I will," returned the other, greatly relieved. "What proof do you require? come, Bob, let's have it."

Old Mr. Coates answered not; but, rising from his seat, he slowly produced from the capacious pocket of his surtout a flat stone jar, that must have contained at least a gallon, and deposited it upon the table with a gravity and solemnity quite imposing.

"I have travelled four-and-twenty miles to procure this," said he. "It's Boyne water, David, and fresh from the scene of King Billy's glory, too—I bottled it myself at half-past ten o'clock this morning exactly opposite the place where his Majesty crossed the river. Come, David, pledge me a bumper of rale Protestant punch made upon this, and I'm satisfied."

"Agreed, Bob," returned Elliott, in high good humour; and, summoning Rody Cormick to his presence, he directed him to boil the water of the Boyne without delay; and so prompt was that person in carrying out his master's wishes, that in an incredibly short time he placed on the hob before them a foaming kettle. Oh, the placidity and happiness that beamed upon old Coates's face, as, leaning back in his chair, he surveyed the bright copper vessel that hummed so cheerily before him, affording promise of plenteous libations of his beloved compound,—King Billy's Cordial!—The sight of it threw him into an ecstacy of delight. Awakening at length from the blissful reverie, he turned to the alderman, and remarked,

"Now do you know, David, that the biling kittle there calls up associations within me of veneration, exultation, and pleasure?"

"Does it, Bob?" returned the alderman, not exactly seeing the matter in the same interesting point of view.

"Why, it reminds one, no doubt, of so much whiskey punch," remarked young Elliott, who had just then entered the room, in a tone of sarcasm that no one could mistake.

"So much whiskey punch!" repeated Mr. Coates, turning contemptuously upon the speaker. "And pray, Sir, do you consave that feelings of veneration could be awakened in my bosom by sperrits and hot water?"

"I haven't said that I conceived anything of the kind," replied the young man, goodhumouredly, as he took a seat by the table.

"And—and—what did you consave, Sir? and what did ye mane by your observation?" asked Mr. Coates, arranging in his mind the programme of his attack, for he intended to come down upon the young man with crushing severity. "Remember, Sir," he added, "'tis Boyne water's in the kittle before us."

"Well, whatever kind of water it is," returned young Elliott, "I fancy it will very soon be affiliated with whiskey and sugar, and that the compound is not destined to be thrown away—is not that so?"

"Is that all, my fine fellow? and does that biling fluid remind you of nothing else?" asked the old gentleman, contemptuously.

"Well, I don't just now see anything more," returned the other, affecting ignorance, though well knowing what old Coates was aiming at; "excepting, indeed, that it might suggest a cheerful cup of tea, when you might throw in a plate of hot muffins; and imagine a group of happy faces round the table, eating and drinking and laughing by turns."

"Ha!—nothing else?" asked Coates, with a short laugh of fearful import.

"Why, to be sure, we might connect it with Watts

and the steam-engine," continued William Nassau, with a thoughtful air; "and then glance off into a reflection upon the effects which steam is probably destined to exercise upon commerce and civilization."

Human nature could bear no more, and Bob was human—

"Boy!" he exclaimed, in a burst of wrath that was sublime in its intensity—"boy! are you not aware that the water which now hisses, boils, and bubbles in that copper cauldron before us, but a few hours ago calmly meandered through the bed of the River Boyne? That fluid, Sir, is sanctified by the blood of the warriors that once ensanguined it, and rendered illustrious by the glorious victory King William won by the river from whence it was procured."

"Why thin, Sir, let me tell ye this," broke in Rody, as he placed "materials" upon the table, "let me tell ye this, that it's mighty bad wather intirely, that same Byne wather, and by no manes aiqual to the wather we get from the fountain in James's-street, God bless it!"

"Hold your tongue, Rody, you don't know what you're talking about," said Alderman Elliott, annoyed at the interruption.

"May be not, Sir," returned Rody, not at all abashed by the rebuke; "but this I know, Sir, that dirtier wather nor that same Byne wather I never see. I declare to ye, Sir, that if I hadn't filthered it through a hair sieve you couldn't swally it, 'twas so filled with little pinkeens and gravel.—No, I don't mind how dry you'd be, nor how mild the sperrits (and betther was never mixed nor what's before ye), you couldn't swally it"—and, placing a large case bottle on the table with a bang, he left the room, evidently the better of having opened his mind.

"I tell you, Master William Nassau," said Bob Coates, resuming his address, "that, ignorant as you are of the elevating influences of Orangeism, you cannot comprehend the high and holy associations connected with that water before us; but I can; yes, and your father can. I fancy now that I see his glorious Majesty, upon the very war-horse that bore him on to victory, charge through the River Boyne, and splash and dash and lash the water about, even as the expanding heat of the fire beneath that kittle agitates and troubles the water within it. Hooray!" exclaimed the enthusiastic old gentleman, warming with his subject—"Hooray!—charge, Billy, charge! On, Scomberg, on! Victory and William the Third for ever! No surrender! and three times three!" And, quite breathless with excitement, Mr. Coates turned to his intended son-in-law to observe the effect his thrilling words had created, but only to his chagrin to find that they threw him into a hearty fit of laughter.

"Young man," exclaimed Coates, his temper rapidly giving way—"young man, your degeneracy grieves, and your flippancy provokes me. I tell you, Sir, that you're a thorn in my side, altho' you may not think so; and there's your worthy father aiqually a martyr. If your heart was in the right place, instead of thinking lightly of it as you do, you'd venerate this fluid for the glorious Battle of the Boyne."

"Pooh! you might as well treasure up some of the water off Cape Trafalgar as a souvenir of Nelson's victory there," was the young man's reply.

"Nonsense, boy, nonsense!" returned old Coates, tartly. "There's no parallel in life between the say fight you allude to and the Battle of the Boyne; besides," he added, as a bright idea flashed upon him, "you couldn't make punch upon say water."

"No, Bob, quite true there—you could not, indeed," broke in the alderman, anxious to afford some encouragement to his old friend, whose temper was undergoing sore trials at the hands of his youthful tormentor.

"And I say, Sir," continued Coates, "that I grieve for your degeneracy. If it were not for you, I wouldn't have gone to the fatague of fetching that water from the County Meath to-day; nor would your father and I have to convert in into whiskey punch, and swallow it afterwards, in order to drown our feelings of sorrow and indignation."

"Oh, Sir, don't subject yourself to so dreadful an ordeal for my sake, I implore of you," exclaimed young Elliott, with apparent concern. "What! get drunk on my account—oh, horrible! Rather than permit it, I'll deprive you of the means"—and, taking the bottle from the table, he moved towards the door.

Poor old Coates's countenance at this juncture wore a dismal expression indeed, and by his *looks* he implored of the young fellow to restore the bottle: but his tormentor was implacable, and only returned with the desired liquor on the request of his father, who was proceeding to rebuke him for his disrespectful conduct, when old Coates interposed, determined to have all the glory himself of crushing his adversary—

"Leave him to me—leave him to me, Davy—I'll settle him!" he exclaimed, intent upon annihilating the offender; when young Elliott—who was now pretty well tired of the subject—with the object of turning the conversation into a more agreeable channel, lost not a moment in introducing the punch. Accordingly, he brewed a reeking jugful, and that too with the famous water in question, and took a wicked pleasure in stirring it up beneath the olfactories of poor Mr. Coates, to the manifest discomposure of that old gentleman, who sniffed up the odour as it ascended, and longed to become better acquainted with it. The thunderbolt he had been forging for the young man's destruction had burst like a bubble: in his eagerness to attack the punch, he had completely forgotten his argument. The alderman, well knowing his kinsman's weakness, now came to his relief—

"Come, William Nassau," said he, in a conciliatory tone, "let us have no more disagreement: so charge the glasses, and join us in the toast which Bob is about to propose."

"With all my heart, Sir," returned the son, filling the glasses, and handing them round.

Bob Coates now rose with dignity, and, nervously

passing his hand across his mouth, proceeded with the toast in question.

"I give you," said he, "'THE GLORIOUS, PIOUS, AND IMMORTAL MEMORY OF THE GREAT AND GOOD KING WILLIAM, WHO SAVED US FROM POPERY, SLAVERY, KNAVERY, BRASS MONEY, WOODEN SHOES, BLACK BREAD, AND ONIONS'!"

"AND CORNS AND BUNIONS," added young Elliott, applying the glass to his lips. His father attempted to follow his example; but, while in the act of doing so, was so much impressed with the ludicrous, at the addenda that had been made to the toast, that he burst into a fit of laughter, and laid down his glass untasted.

Never did Bob Coates display greater dignity and firmness than on this occasion. Placing his tumbler on the table (which however he had previously emptied), he turned upon the delinquent, and demanded an explanation of his conduct, while his countenance wore an expression of severity that alone was sufficient to crush any adversary—

"I look upon your conduct, Sir, as a direct insult to your father and myself," said he. "What! to tack on a low vulgar doggrel to the loyal toast I proposed,—a toast that has been drunk and honoured for generations past by the noblest in the land. 'BLACK BREAD AND ONIONS!—CORNS AND BUNIONS'!" he repeated. "Explain yourself, Sir"—and in the height of his indignation he poured himself out another bumper, and drank it on the instant.

"Why, Sir, I am surprised at your anger," replied young Elliott, with admirable gravity; "the words I added are appropriate, and, in point of fact, the toast is *lame* without them. If King William protected us from the infliction of wearing wooden shoes, did he not also save us from their concomitants,—corns, bunions, and what not? Were we obliged to wear wooden shoes, we should be worse off than the ladies of China; a well-shaped foot would be a curiosity, and the best trade going would be corn curing; therefore I emphatically repeat that we owe our freedom from these dreadful evils to King William, who saved us, as you assure us, from wearing wooden shoes."

Staggered with the force of these remarks, but by no means convinced of the young man's sincerity, Bob Coates scrutinized the latter's visage attentively,—an ordeal which young Elliott bore unflinchingly. Satisfied now at his young friend's seriousness, he became convinced of the force of his argument. "By Jove, William Nassau, you're right," said he, shaking the young man warmly by the hand; you're right, my boy; I never before saw the matter in the light you put it: I'll take a note of your observation, and mention it to the brethren to-morrow. Yes, to be sure, King William did save us from corns and bunions; and, as the last toast goes for nothing, why, we'll adopt your suggestion this very moment in a fresh one. Come, fill the glasses;" and, uttering a sonorous hem! he arose, and gave the amended toast with all the dignity and importance it demanded. "Hip, hip, hooray!" and down went the contents of the glasses; and it is but justice to say that, on this occasion, young Elliott afforded Mr. Coates the most complete satisfaction. His father, however, did not do so, and Bob Coates expressed himself quite dissatisfied with his conduct.

"Davy," said he, as he peered with hungry lips into the alderman's tumbler, which was only partially empty, "this won't do at all. There's not half the old fire in you, for you do not dispose of your liquor in the same loyal style at all that you used. Your behaviour reminds me forcibly of the witness who kissed his thumb in order to escape the oath. I may be wrong, but it's no harm to try again. Come now, no heel-taps!" so the glasses once more were charged; and this time old Coates was fully satisfied. "And now, David, my boy," said the veteran toper, "'tis your turn now to propose a toast: come, let's have the good old one; it warms my heart to hear it uttered."

"Which do you mean, Bob?" asked the alderman, filling up his glass, preparatory to complying with the request.

"Number three, of course; 'the Constitution,'" returned Coates, refreshing his friend's memory. "First, 'the King;' next, 'the Glorious, Pious;' and then, 'the Constitution;' that's the right order of succession, you know."

"Oh! yes, to be sure," responded Elliott, rising briskly from his seat, and holding forth his punch glass, while with admirable solemnity of voice and aspect he gave the cabalistic toast of "*The Constitution, the whole Constitution, and nothing but the Constitution,*" which was drunk not only by the two Orangemen, but by young Elliott also, with the utmost enthusiasm. The apparent fervour of the young man quite overpowered old Mr. Coates, who, unable to contain his emotion, clasped him to his bosom, exclaiming at intervals, while tears of gladness glistened in his bloodshot eyes, "God bless you, my dear young friend; God bless you, my boy; you'll prove an ornament yet to the cause, and an honour to your race. You see, David, he is coming round—he's coming round," said he, addressing the alderman, and intimating in doing so that the film which had obscured young Elliott's mental vision was clearing away, and that he was awakening at length to the glories and advantages appertaining to the Orange system.

The delight of the father at this happy state of things was very great indeed. "Bill, my boy, I am proud of you," said he, pressing his son's hand, while visibly affected; "God bless you, my son," and, by way of subduing his emotion, he raised his glass to his lips, and drained it in a draught.

"Well, I'm very glad I have pleased you, Sir," returned the young man; "but now I hope you'll enlighten me as to what the toast we have just drank signifies; for, although I have heard it more than once before, I protest I am still entirely ignorant of its meaning."

This declaration sadly damped the premature joy of the brethren, whose disappointment was plainly expressed in the many significant glances they interchanged. Like King Pharaoh of old, young Elliott's heart remained still hardened.

"Well, what *does* the toast mean?" repeated the young man, finding that neither of the brethren had ventured upon an explanation.

"What does it mean!—William Nassau, I'm surprised at you," returned the alderman, evidently in some perplexity himself upon the subject; "why, it means—yes, to be sure it does—the Constitution;" and he looked for confirmation to his kinsman, Bob Coates, who, quite concurring in the other's definition, nodded his head in token of approval.

"The Constitution means the Constitution," returned young Elliott, drily; "surely, that affords no information. I'm just as much at sea as ever."

"Why, of course it does—what else would it mean—eh, Bob?" and the alderman again appealed for assistance to Brother Coates.

"Certainly—what else?" returned the gentleman appealed to; "it signifies the Constitution, with King William and all that sort of thing," and the Orangemen smiled complacently at each other, and sipped their punch with the satisfied air of men who had skilfully clenched a difficult argument, and completely silenced their antagonist.

Young Elliott, however, who was not to be so easily disposed of, now assured the brethren that they had not at all enlightened his darkness, and that he was still in perfect ignorance as to what the words "the Constitution, the whole Constitution, and nothing but the Constitution," meant; and, putting his question into a more definite form, he again sought for a solution. Old Mr. Coates now, in obedience to a request from the alderman, entered upon an elaborate explanation, in the course of which he got so completely out of his depth, and found himself entangled in such an inextricable web of confusion, that the poor old gentleman quite forgot from whence he had started, or indeed what the object of his attempted explanation was; and, in his embarrassment and confusion, applied so frequently for inspiration to the bottle, that young Elliott, in sheer pity, came to his relief, by assuring him that it was unnecessary to proceed further, as he was now completely satisfied on the subject. And indeed such was the case; for Bob Coates's rambling and incoherent statement had proved to him beyond doubt that the enthusiastic old Orangeman was quite as ignorant of the meaning of the toast in question as he was himself. The old fellow, however, in the course of his wild rhapsody, had succeeded in impressing him with the fact, that, in common with the rest of the Orangemen, he contemplated with steadfast faith the establishment in this country at some future day of an Utopian kingdom, or millennium, presided over by a prince devoted to the Orange cause, in which Orangemen only should be admitted to the dignity of citizenship, and when all who were not orthodox Protestants should be either extirpated from the land, or allowed to exist on sufferance only, to serve as "hewers of wood and drawers of water."

Alderman Elliott was greatly pleased at the success with which, as he conceived, his kinsman had explained the matter, and by way of evincing his satisfaction urged Bob Coates to apply himself more vigorously to the bottle,—an invitation which the jolly old drunkard was by no means slow to avail himself of, as the frequency with which he helped himself to the fiery fluid abundantly testified.

CHAPTER IV.

"Drink and speak, parrot; and squabble, swagger, swear, and discourse fustian with one's own shadow. Oh, thou invisible spirit of wine, if thou hast none other name to be known by, let's call thee—devil! . . . . Oh that men should put an enemy into their mouths to steal away their brains; that we should with joy, revel, pleasure, and applause, transform ourselves into beasts."

As it was now pretty clear that the brethren were intent upon a carouse, young Elliott, who was of temperate habits, thought it prudent to retire. His father and Bob Coates pressed him to remain, but he declined to do so, fearing to trust himself longer with men of such tried and unshaken loyalty, and of such extraordinary powers of absorption. Left thus to their punch and their loyalty, the brethren proceeded to enjoy themselves in real downright earnest; so they drank and chatted away, occasionally relieving the monotony by indulging in "loyal toasts," such as would amuse the curious from their original and farfetched character, and in stray snatches of song, expressive, of course, of their unswerving loyalty to the British Crown, and their determination to crush and keep down the Pope and his adherents. Throughout all this conviviality, however,

Bob Coates never lost sight of the main point, but constantly brought round the subject to the perilous position of young Elliott—

"Now, Davy, my dear friend, you must positively put a stop to this courtship at once," said he, when he considered he had rendered the alderman sufficiently plastic for his purpose. "Hang it! I feel some way or other quite like a second father for William Nassau; he's a fine handsome young fellow, and it would be a sin and a scandal to allow him to fall into the snares of that crafty young Delilah yonder, whose meretricious charms appear to have dazzled his boyish fancy."

"I tell you, Bob, you need be under no apprehensions on the subject," interrupted Elliott: "I have forbidden William Nassau to marry the girl, and I am sure he will not disobey me; so make your mind easy—for so long as David Elliott is above ground he will not allow the blood of his ancestors to be profaned."

"Bless you, Davy—bless you!" returned Coates, wringing his kinsman's hand with strong emotion; "you have removed a heavy load from my heart,—yet still there is one precaution I would advise you to adopt."

"Out with it, Bob!" was the alderman's reply, as he helped himself to a fresh supply of King Billy's Cordial.

"I tell you what it is," returned Coates, speaking in a subdued voice, but with great deliberation, "I would have you call upon the mother of this young famale, and come to a proper understanding with her. Trust me, she can very easily put a stop to the courtship that's going on, if she likes: why not send her daughter out of the way, I ask?"

This suggestion met with the cordial approval of the alderman, who assured his friend that he would not fail to act upon it, and that accordingly he would wait upon the Widow Lonergan on the subject.

"Don't lose a day in doing so—every hour's delay is fraught with dangerous consequences," returned Coates.

"I'll call upon her, please God, to-morrow," said Elliott, "and lay the whole case before her. It's just possible," he added, a new light seeming to burst upon him, "that she has never received the letter I wrote her, for the girl herself may have intercepted it."

"Exactly so," returned Bob Coates, briskly; "I'll lay a small wager the widow never saw your letter at all. Young famales like her are so full of artifice, that I'm confident she was on the watch, and the moment she got possession of it destroyed it. But you can set all right on an interview with her mother. Spake firmly, but very respectfully, to her. Tell her that, apart from the girl being a Papist, and all belonging to her, she is no match for a son of your's, and that she must look somewhere else for a son-in-law; and, my life upon it, you'll soon put an extinguisher upon the affair. As for William Nassau, we can have no difficulty in providing him with a suitable partner, who will amply console him for the one he'll have lost—

"There are Protestant maidens more lovely by far,
Who would gladly be bride to the young Lochinvar."

And the sly old fox screwed up one eye, and surveyed his kinsman anxiously with the other. He had thrown out a strong hint in favour of his daughter, which he doubted not his friend would act upon at once. He was disappointed, however, for the alderman made no sign, and the hint, strong though it was, fell useless to the ground. Finding that his friend was abstracted, and not likely to avail himself of his suggestions, he thought it better not to waste his ammunition further, but to wait for another occasion, when he could make his missiles go home with effect to the mark.

"Yes, Bob, I'll call upon the Widow Lonergan to-morrow," said Elliott, "and I'll clench the business for ever."

"Bravo! Davy, bravo!" exclaimed old Coates, emptying his tumbler at a draught, and rapturously shaking his kinsman's hand. "All right and tight, my boy! that's the way to do business, Davy."

"Ay, ay, I think so," returned his friend, looking around triumphantly.

Having now got the alderman into a pliable humour, or, in other words, pretty nearly "half seas over," Bob Coates determined to make the most of his opportunity, and to extort a promise from his friend to give his brother Orangemen a grand dinner, or, as he was in the habit of terming such, "a jollification;" for truth obliges us to add that old Coates was an epicure and a glutton, as well as a drunkard, and dearly loved "the pleasures of the table"—as indulgence in the good things of this life has been termed—which his own limited means precluded him from indulging in to the extent he desired. The wily old fellow made his approaches skilfully, and succeeded, as will be seen, to the full extent of his expectations—

"Davy," said he, "I've a favour to ask from you, which I know you'll comply with—in fact, it's due to yourself to do so."

"Let's hear it, old boy," returned the alderman, poking up the fire goodhumouredly.

"Well, the fact is," continued Coates, "I've as good as promised some of the brethren that you mean to give them a dinner soon—a rale right down loyal affair, you know—such as will prove beyond all question that, however William Nassau may have acted, you are true blue yourself to the back bone."

"If that's all the favour you ask, Bob, 'tis granted at once. I'll give you such a spread, Sir, as will surprise and astonish you all. Give a dinner!" repeated the alderman; "you shall have such a banquet, Sir, as shall become a household word in the Lodge; for I'll lay you all up for a month after it; and as for yourself, I'll give you a fit of the gout, my boy." And, greatly to old Coates's delight, he touched him jocularly in the ribs, throwing him into a fit of mingled coughing and laughter that threatened to be attended with dangerous consequences. Having with some difficulty recovered himself, the old fellow crowed aloud with joy, and gleefully rubbed his hands together, as if the impending fit of the gout was a blessing to be highly appreciated, continuing to exclaim at intervals—"Davy, my boy, I've hopes for you yet—yes, ha! ha! ha!—I've hopes for you still."

"Well, Bob, we'll consider the dinner a settled thing," said the alderman: "so now let us be jolly. How stands the Boyne water?"

"There are two good quarts of it yet," replied Coates, weighing the kettle in his hand. "And I earnestly entreat that we shall not desecrate the blessed fluid by applying it to base purposes. Only consave a servant making tay or biling eggs with Boyne water: the very idaya is disgusting. Let's conshume it all in the same loyal style we've begun. It's an immense thing to do, to be sure; but, for all that, let's go through it like men. Let us turn it all into Protestant punch."

"By all means, Bob,—so let us make a night of it," was the willing response. And we are bound to add that they did make a night of it, and a morning also, for they did not separate until the small hours were pretty far advanced; when, we regret to add, the worthy alderman was in a condition decidedly unbecoming a respectable burgess holding the dignified position that he did; but as for his companion, it was a miracle that he retained his perpendicular.

"Good nigh—t!——Bl—less you! bl—less you, Davy!" uttered the old toper, as, while "willing to go, but yet loth to depart," he still lingered on the threshold. "Bl—less you! and mind," he added, for, though drunk as Bacchus, the old fellow had his wits about him—"mind now, Davy, don't forget—to call upon the widow."

"Never fear me, Bob, I'll wait upon her to-morrow," said the alderman, the recollection of the important duty before him restoring him to some degree of steadiness.

"And settle everything—eh? Davy," asked Bob Coates.

"Yes, Bob, I'll settle everything, depend upon it."

"All right and tight, my boy,—that's what I call bizz—bizz—buisness," returned Coates, shutting one eye, and pressing his forefinger to the side of his nose; by which performance, though he intended to look remarkably knowing, he only succeeded in getting up a drunken leer,—which thoroughly satisfied the other, far gone as he was, that Coates was all but in the last stage of intoxication. And the old fellow jogged homewards, hiccuping as he went, and singing at the top of his voice the Orange ditty,

"July the First, in Oldbridge Town, there was a famous battle;"

or rather attempting to do so, for he never got beyond the first line.

CHAPTER V.

"She was a phantom of delight,
When first she gleamed upon my sight:
A lovely apparition, sent
To be a moment's ornament;
Her eyes as stars of twilight fair;
Like twilight's, too, her dusky hair;
But all things else about her drawn
From May-time and the cheerful dawn;
A dancing shape, an image gay,
To haunt, to startle, and waylay."

THE ensuing morning Alderman Elliott arose, strong in his magnanimous determination of calling upon the Widow Lonergan, and putting an end to all further intercourse between their respective children. Having been occupied with business the early part of the day, he postponed his visit until the afternoon,—an arrangement which suited him admirably, as, after disposing of affairs at the widow's, he had only to proceed from thence to the Lodge, and inform Mr. Coates and the rest of the brethren of the result of his interview. We accordingly find the worthy alderman at about seven o'clock in the evening knocking at Mrs. Lonergan's door with all the gravity and solemnity that the occasion demanded. The widow happened at the time to be engaged with customers in her shop, in which she carried on an extensive business; for in those days there were no monster drapery establishments such as there are at present, which, like Aaron's rod, swallow up all the rest, and leave no chance for the industrious small trader to eke out a livelihood. The servant accordingly invited him to enter, and await her mistress's coming. David Elliott was loth to enter this stronghold of Popery and treason; his desire was to have met the widow on the threshold, and have there disposed of his business without entering her house. As it was, however, he had no alternative but to do as the servant had requested. The room he was shown into, which was comfortably and even elegantly furnished, had for him a novelty and freshness about it that surprised and pleased him. Everything around bespoke the civilizing presence of woman: the vase of flowers on the table, which enriched the air with perfume, and the numerous other elegancies and pleasing trifles which the refined taste of woman delights in surrounding her home with, seemed to shed a halo of peace and happiness around him. There was a range of books in a cabinet to which his attention was attracted: here he expected to find disloyalty and ultramonantism in its most revolting form. He read over the names:—"*The Life of Charles the Twelfth;*" "*The Mysteries of Udolpho;*" "*Every one his own Gardener;*" "*Robinson Crusoe;*" "*Miss Edgeworth's Tales of Fashionable Life;*" and a few more of the same diversified class. There was no volume of a sectarian character amongst them; and the alderman, in his own words, was "surprised and astonished." He turned to the scrap-book that lay open upon the table, and to his surprise found that it contained none of the offensive caricatures of public characters which in those days the print shops teemed with, most of them being directed against the members of the Dublin Corporation and the Orange body to which he belonged. The piano lay open, with a piece of music upon it, as if the notes had just thrilled to the touch of its presiding genius; he ran his hands listlessly over the notes, and the familiar sounds recalled the memories of other days, and brought a pleasing sadness to his heart. He thought of his own expensive "Broadwood" at home, which, not having been opened for years, lay neglected, aside, dusty and gloomy, like a coffin waiting to receive its tenant; while the hands "that had waked it so often" were long crumbled with their kindred dust. He paced the room, and sighed; yet his feelings were of a pleasurable kind. The object of his visit for the time was forgotten; and the memories of bygone years crowded upon his mind.

Mrs. Lonergan remained away a long time, and David Elliott took a seat on a sofa, as one will do who feels himself at home. Those who have passed years of their lives in wild and uncultivated scenes with rough and rude companions, and then, on returning to civilized life, enter some home, such as a mother, a sister, or a wife may have once graced with her presence, can form some idea of the pleasing though undefinable feelings that possessed him. Oh, how his own dull lonely house, that never echoed to a woman's laugh, stood out before him in gloomy contrast to this! He thought of the time when a young and gentle wife, long passed away from him, cheered his path through the world, and made his home a peaceful and a happy one,—when his evenings, instead of being wasted as now in carousing and drunken revelry, were passed in a home like this, sanctified by the presence of that pure and loving wife, and gladdened by her smiles and converse; —yes, those were happy days.

Having abandoned himself to reflections like these, he awoke from his reverie, and, suffering his eyes to roam through the room, was attracted to the portrait of a young and handsome female, admirably executed in oil, the features of which at once brought before him the young girl he had seen in company with his son in the theatre. This at once recalled him to the reality of his position, and, rising from his seat, he approached the picture with the view of examining it more closely—"This must be the young girl who is doing all the mischief," said he, as he closely scrutinized the portrait. "Yes; and after all I must own that Bill has good taste."—The term by which he had thus designated his son was that which he usually applied to him when he was particularly pleased with him.—"Yes," he continued, "Bill has decidedly good taste; she's not quite so young as I thought she was, but she's a dashing fine girl for all that; she has figure and fulness without coarseness, and there's a spark of fun in those fine dark eyes of hers that pleases me vastly." He had proceeded thus far, when he heard the sound of approaching footsteps; the next moment he turned round, and Mrs. Lonergan herself stood before him. Now, the widow was a remarkably fine woman, no one could venture to deny it. Her eyes were dark blue, large and lustrous; with an animation and softness, expressive at once of intelligence, cheerfulness, and good nature. Her hair was almost raven-black, and she had a profusion of it, but she partially concealed it beneath a coquettish little cap that would make the plainest face look positively handsome; her features were regular, and blended together with wondrous harmony; her complexion, clear as Parian marble, was relieved by a delicate tinge of carmine, that lent expression to her eyes, and lighted up her countenance with a brilliancy rendering her at times dazzlingly beautiful. Her figure was tall and graceful; and she had a foot and ankle that Canova might have dreamed of, but could never fashion. Had her lot been cast amongst the magnates of the land, she would have been toasted and celebrated as a beauty; but, belonging only to the trading classes, who value more the useful than the beautiful, she was only known to her own narrow circle, and even there her loveliness did not meet the appreciation it deserved. She was indeed a splendid specimen of womankind; and one could not behold her without applying to her the lines that Dr. Johnson penned to his friend Mrs. Thrale :—

"That whosoe'er would wish to wive
Should look on her at thirty-five."

So great, indeed, was the sensation she created whenever she appeared amongst the male creation, that it has been declared by competent authority that the blaze of her charms has caused Dr. O'Flynn himself—that austere and stern man—even in his most cynical moments, to avert his eyes, and look down at his boots in confusion. The portrait which had engaged Mr. Elliott's attention in fact was hers, having been taken a few years earlier, when she was little more than thirty years of age; for, having been married when a mere girl, she was now scarcely six and thirty. Our hero, as he surveyed the widow, was at a complete *non plus*. She was hardly young enough, and seemed too mature for the daughter, although she strikingly brought that young lady before him; and it was quite out of the question, he thought, that she could be the widow herself. Yet she must be either. Whoever she was, it was quite clear she was the original of the picture he had been contemplating. "It must be the daughter," thought he, "and I'll address her accordingly. If I am correct, there will be no harm done; and if I should be wrong, and she turns out to be the mother, I'll have paid her a compliment that cannot fail to be appreciated." These thoughts passed rapidly through his mind as he surveyed the lady, preparatory to introducing himself to her. It will thus be seen that the charming face and figure of the widow had made a strong impression upon him. In accordance with the course he had decided upon, he bowed to the widow with a respectfully gallantry that became him admirably, and asked "had he the pleasure of seeing *Miss* Lonergan?"

"No, Sir, you see her mother," replied the widow,

smiling sweetly, and displaying as she did so two strings of pearls, relieved by lips so ripe and rosy as quite ravished poor Alderman Elliott. He was right, however;—his compliment had told forcibly; for there breathes not the woman who is insensible to flattery, when the tribute either has or *appears* to have been involuntarily bestowed; nor is there any more effectual receipt for putting a pretty woman into good humour with herself and all mankind, than a little flattery skilfully administered, but there lies all the difficulty.

"No, Sir, you see her mother," said the widow.

"Bless my heart and soul! I'm surprised and astonished," returned Mr. Elliott, ingenuously — "why, Ma'am, I have been admiring you for the past five minutes without knowing it," and he waved his hand toward the portrait.

This remarkable speech, and the *naïvété* with which it was uttered, proceeding from a middle-aged gentleman of the dignified appearance of the alderman, proved so entertaining to the widow, who was full of vivacity, that, dropping into a seat, she burst into a hearty fit of laughter, which at first rather disconcerted the alderman, but who, catching the contagion, as it were, soon joined her with right good will.

"And, pray, who is my admirer?" asked the widow, when her merriment had subsided.

"Alderman Elliott, Ma'am, your near neighbour," returned our hero, bowing and smirking, and looking by no means the steady, sensible character he was generally considered.

"Alderman Elliott!" thought the widow, "the very person who wrote me such a serious letter about Kate; what can this visit mean?" and the poor lady, greatly alarmed, begged of her visitor to be seated, with a gravity of demeanour that contrasted strangely with her previous gaiety.

"Thank you, Ma'am," said the alderman, accepting the widow's invitation, and looking straight in her face. Now it so happened that Mrs. Lonergan never looked lovelier than at this moment. When such a man as Dr. O'Flynn could not gaze upon her charms without wincing, how could poor Mr. Elliott, whose heart was naturally a susceptible one, go through the ordeal unscathed? He could not, nor did he indeed make any effort to do so. In fact, he became a willing victim, and succumbed, completely subdued by the fascinations of the young and blooming widow. A silence of some moments ensued, during which the alderman collected his thoughts, and summoned courage to speak; but, instead of entering upon the object of his mission, as the lady evidently expected, he glanced off upon another subject, which she was entirely unprepared for.

"Excuse me now, Ma'am, for putting the question," said he, "but do you know what I have been thinking of?"

"How should I know, Sir?" returned the widow, smiling sweetly, and again displaying those pearly teeth that positively brought the water into Mr. Elliott's.

"Well, Ma'am, it has just occurred to me," continued the alderman, "that I have been the most stupid of men, to have had so beautiful a woman as you living near me, and to have been ignorant of the fact until now."

"Oh, Sir, you are pleased to flatter," replied the widow, blushing a deeper carmine, and looking more bewitching than before. In truth, she was so much confused and abashed at the language and the earnest gaze of her visitor, in whose countenance admiration was unmistakeably depicted, that she was unable adequately to express herself.

"No, Ma'am, I respectfully deny that I flatter you," returned the alderman. "Flattery, my dear Madam, is but gilded falsehood; while what I state is the plain, unvarnished truth, which no man need be afraid or ashamed to utter; and I say again, that I never dreamt there was so much beaúty near me, much less in your person, Ma'am. Before I had the pleasure of seeing you, I looked upon that portrait as your daughter's—for I have seen the young lady before—but I find now it is your own, and that you have the advantage of her."

Just at this moment it happened that the young girl referred to—intent upon preparations for the evening's meal—was about to enter the room, but, hearing voices within, she paused for a moment on the threshold, and heard the allusion made to her, which, though flattering to her mother, was not complimentary to herself. "Who can he be?" she thought; then impelled by curiosity, she advanced into the room, and recognised the father of her lover.

"Kate, dear, this is Alderman Elliott," said the widow, introducing our hero, who quite familiarly held out his hand to her.

"And so you think, Sir, that my mother has the advantage of me," said Kate, giving him her hand, and looking archly in his face.

The alderman, who now recognised her, attempted to enter upon an explanation, which the young lady interrupting, continued—

"You can't deny it, Sir, for I heard you as I was entering the room. But let me tell you, Sir, that I don't think she has," and she tossed her head, shook her curls, and worked up her pretty face into an expression of assumed anger, that quite entertained him. The young girl, with the tact and quickness of her sex, having seen in a moment the happy aspect of affairs, had determined to turn it to the most profitable account.

"My dear young lady," said the alderman, growing quite gallant on the occasion, "you must pardon my hasty remark, for I made it in complete ignorance of the fact; but now that I see your blooming face, I retract what I have stated, and declare you to be a captivating, charming girl: quite a second edition of your mother; and the second edition, you know, is always an improvement on the first."

The alderman was making rapid progress in the art of love; in propitiating the daughter, he had levelled a compliment at the mother, having much meaning and significancy in it.

"Oh, that is all very well," continued Kate, still

affecting displeasure, though really in a perfect rapture of delight; "but you know you've been convicted of slander—a breach of gallantry I cannot overlook; however, as it's your first offence, I'll allow what you have urged to go in mitigation of punishment."

"Well, what is to be the infliction?" asked the gentleman, greatly amused at the young lady's speech, and the air with which she delivered it.

"I sentence you to imprisonment, with hard labour," she continued, with the same serio-comic tone.

"What can you mean, Kate?" asked her mother, growing alarmed at her daughter's freedom towards so great a man as their visitor.

"Imprisonment, with hard labour!" exclaimed the alderman, enjoying the scene vastly; "that's a severe sentence to pass upon me."

"Not half what you deserve," said Kate; "for I only intend to incarcerate you for this evening—your prison shall be this house; and as for the hard labour, it shall consist in drinking tea with us,"—so saying, the lively young girl seized his hat and umbrella, and left him standing irresolute in the centre of the room. The widow having now added her invitation to her daughter's, Mr. Elliott did not hesitate a moment in accepting their hospitality; and in a few moments he found himself seated at the table with the tea equipage temptingly displayed before him—supplemented on the occasion by a plate of that favourite comestible familiarly known to the good people of Dublin as "hot cake," and made too by Catherine's own dainty hands. Never, surely, was more endurable punishment meted out to erring man. Poor Kate was so elated with joy at the alderman's unexpected visit, and the bright prospect of future happiness it opened out to her, that her spirits rose to the height of exuberance. Her heart so warmed to our hero, that she would have loaded him with kindness. Had it been a dog of her lover's that had come to her door, she would have welcomed it with caresses for his sake: how greatly, then, was she delighted to have his father for her guest! She was not, however, more happy, it will be seen, than Mr. Elliott was on the occasion. As the reader can very well imagine, the alderman was not a tea-drinking man, yet now he drank several cupsful. When the meal was over, Kate took her seat at the piano, and played with skill some popular airs, many of which Elliott had heard in happier days now long past; and the familiar sounds vibrated to his heart, and released a flood of early associations within him, that refreshed him, and made him feel a better man.

> "Like the gale that sighs along
> Beds of oriental flowers,
> Is the grateful breath of song
> That once was heard in happier hours."

Kate, full of hope, and all life and spirits, now left the piano, and, taking a seat between her seniors, never allowed the conversation to flag for a moment; so that between her vivacity and the fascinations of the widow, Mr. Elliott entirely lost sight of the weighty business that had brought him to the house; or, if he thought of it, he did so only to guard himself from allowing his entertainers to suspect what the burden of it was. Thus the evening wore round,—his heart escaping from him every moment until scarce a shred of it remained. Eleven o'clock came: the very hour when he should be in the midst of his brethren, venting his loyalty and imbibing his punch, yet there he was, sitting opposite the widow, whose bright eyes, like the sun reflected from a mirror, so fascinated and dazzled him, and rendered him so unconscious of everything save her transcendant charms, that he never counted time, nor even thought of "the Lodge." When he bade the widow good night, and she placed her small white hand in his, he was attacked with a palpitation, or a kind of fluttering rather, about his heart, that quite took his speech away; however, his looks made up for words; and, to do the lady justice, her's were equally expressive—for the alderman, though no longer young, was a fine-looking fellow, with a frank, lively manner that wins a lady's favour, and had made, it could be clearly seen, a decided impression on the widow. Kate now brought him his hat quite attentively, and forgave him for alluding so disparagingly to her charms, but admonished him to be more cautious in future. Taking one of her hands in his, and looking benignly in her face, Mr. Elliott assured her, with a significance of expression the young girl well understood, that she should not again have occasion to scold him; and, stooping down, he imprinted a paternal kiss on her smooth, fair brow, upon which purity and truth were imprinted by God's own handywork, and once more bade her and her mother good night.

"Bless my heart and soul!" exclaimed the alderman, when the hall door had closed upon him—"I am surprised and astonished; what a stupid man I have been, never to have mentioned a word of the business I called about. Bob Coates will never forgive me. But stay.—By Jove, I have it; I have left my umbrella behind me, and I'll just step back for it, and mention the matter." Oh, the deceitfulness of the human heart! He was only anxious to feast his eyes with one more glance at the lovely widow; yet he would cozen himself into the belief that he wanted to return for the purpose of falling out with her. So strong was his desire to see her once more, that his hand was on the point of raising the knocker, when wiser thoughts possessed him.—"No," said he, "it's too late, now; I'll return for my umbrella to-morrow." And the alderman bent his footsteps towards home.

"Well, I suppose you've settled all that," remarked young Elliott to his father, as he opened the hall door to admit him; for he was aware of the visit he had made, and the object of it.

"Yes, I've been at Mrs. Lonergan's till now," returned the alderman; "and I've settled everything."

"You were a very long time about it," observed the young man, drily; but his father, not thinking it worth while to reply, went up straightway to bed.

CHAPTER VI.

"Marriage is a matter of more worth,
Than to be dealt with by attorneyship.
*   *   *   *
For what is wedlock forced but a hell,
An age of discord and continual strife?
Whereas the contrary bringeth forth bliss,
And is a pattern of celestial peace."

THE evening following the events just treated of, Mrs. Lonergan received a visit from her spiritual adviser, Father O'Flynn. There was a frown upon his brow, and the widow trembled; for her practised eye assured her that this mark of displeasure portended an outburst of wrath she knew not how to cope with or endure. Returning her welcome with a cool and scanty greeting, the doctor took a chair in silence, while his stifled breathing more eloquently than words confirmed the lady's apprehensions.

"And so, I find, you haven't yet put a stop to the intercourse between your daughter and that heretic young man opposite," said he, entering at once upon the object of his visit, and looking sternly at the widow, who, confident that he was aware of Alderman Elliott's visit of the previous evening, almost lost the use of speech with terror, and did not attempt a reply; for such intimacy with a person of Elliott's principles would be condemned, she knew, by his reverence as an unpardonable crime.

"I have it," continued the doctor, in allusion to the lovers, "that it's at the play they were not three weeks ago, and that they have since been seen constantly together. Who my informant is I really do not know, for he modestly withholds his name from the letters he sends me; but, whoever he is, there can be no doubt he is a good Catholic, and a great deal more anxious for the honour of your family than you are yourself, Mrs. Lonergan."

"I am sure I have done everything in my power to dissuade Kate from associating with young Mr. Elliott," returned the widow, dissolving into tears, which should have melted the heart of his reverence, but did not. "I have lectured her, and scolded her, and—and she's a disobedient girl."

"Where is Catherine now?" asked the doctor, unheeding the widow's tribulation.

"I don't know, indeed," she returned, applying her handkerchief to her eyes.

"Of course you don't," rejoined his reverence, sarcastically; "but maybe others know. What would you think, Ma'am, if you heard that your daughter has just been seen in company with the young man I speak of, and they walking arm-in-arm together, no less? You're a pretty sample of a pious Catholic, Mrs. Lonergan!"

To these taunts the widow did not reply; and there is no doubt the doctor would have administered some further reproofs of a more severe and cutting nature, had not Catherine herself arrived upon the scene, and diverted his wrath from her mother to herself. She had just returned from a walk with her lover in the suburbs, and the fresh air and exercise had lent a bloom to her face that rendered her the very impersonation of youth, health, and loveliness.

"Come here, girl," said the doctor, relaxing none of his severity. "Answer me now, without fencing or evasion,—have you, or have you not, been in company with that heretic youth opposite?"

"Young Mr. Elliott, you mean?" asked Catherine, with coolness; for there was an acerbity in the doctor's tone that roused her courage, and determined her not to submit to him with tameness.

"Yes, I do," returned the doctor, sharply.

"Why, Sir, we have only just parted," returned Kate, with a candour that quite disconcerted her questioner; and, throwing herself into a seat, she removed her bonnet, allowing a cluster of rich dark hair to flow in luxurious abundance around her rosy face, from whence a pair of bright eyes surveyed his reverence with an archness that would have rendered her an admirable study for a painter. Then, arising from her seat, she added—"And look, Sir, at the beautiful bouquet he has given me," and she placed the flowers beneath his reverence's nose.

"Faugh! take them away," said the doctor, "they smell of——

"Roses," said Catherine, completing the sentence, and placing the flowers in her bosom.

"Girl!" continued the doctor, with solemnity, but with less of his former severity, "you are entering upon the broad road that leads all who journey by it to destruction. Remember that they who do not hearken to the warning voice of the Church disregard the injunctions of Heaven. You must give up this young man, or he'll pervert and corrupt you, and lead you a wanderer from the fold, so that you'll find yourself at last forsaken by God, and neglected by the world. You must neither walk with him, nor hold converse with him."

"I am sure I can see no harm in walking with him, nor in talking to him either," returned Kate, quickly, while a flush of anger mounting to her face marred for the instant all its sweetness and serenity. The transition was but momentary; for, remembering the respect due to the doctor's character and calling, and conscious also of the goodness of his intentions, all feelings of resentment vanished; while the thought that it was ungrateful and unmaidenly to harbour angry feelings towards him, caused a blush to mantle to her cheeks, that suffused her face and neck with crimson.

"Harm!" exclaimed the doctor, throwing up the whites of his eyes in horror, and quite unconscious of the feelings that pervaded his young friend's bosom. "No, child; nor there's no harm in walking with Satan, if you don't go home with him, and do as he prompts you. Harm! Why, child, admitting you remained faithful to the Church, which is exceedingly problematical, only imagine yourself the wife of this young heretic, and in course of time the mother of seven, or eight, or ten, ay, or fourteen, or eighteen, or may be twenty young Elliotts, all going, as assuredly they would, to the wrong place—every one of them Protestants, like their father, or may be Orangemen, like their reprobate grandfather. Why, 'tis robbing the Church of her children you'd be." His reverence had got thus far, when the object of his admonition, with the view of averting his wrath, took her seat by the piano, and began to sing in a subdued tone one of the doctor's favourite melodies with a sweetness that at another time would have softened his heart, but which now had only the effect of adding fuel to his anger.

"What! you disregard me," he exclaimed; "and you persist in linking your fate with one whom the Church condemns. Well, be it so; but you'll repent of it yet, child, in sackcloth and ashes." Then, relaxing slightly his severity, he continued—"Do you not know, Catherine, that this young boy you profess such a silly fancy for is a heretic, and out of the pale of the Holy Catholic Church, and that heretics cannot enter the kingdom of heaven? And do you not know, child, that his whole family—his breed, seed, and generation, as it were—are heretics also; and that his father is one, too, of the deepest dye,—a man whose case we regard as hopeless,—for no one ever heard of an Orangeman like him conforming to Catholicity. The Church, in fact, wouldn't take a present of such a man. He's doomed, child—he's doomed; and as sure as I now speak to you, the name of Elliott the Orangeman is already registered in the booking-office below;"—and Doctor O'Flynn struck the floor with his stick, and pointed downward with awful significance.

Here the widow—who, having quite recovered from her grief, had been listening for some time with close attention to the doctor's ghostly admonition—remarked with feeling, "that she'd be sorry to think Alderman Elliott should go *there* (meaning the dreaded region indicated by his reverence), as a nicer man she never saw."

Doctor O'Flynn was in splendid trim for argument this evening. Turning full upon the widow, his countenance animated with a wicked gleam of triumph, indicating clearly that he felt he had her in his power, and that it was not his intention to allow her to escape too easily, he demanded had she anything more to say in favour of the alderman? to which having received no response, he continued—

"A nice man you call him,—and you'd be sorry to think he'd go there, would you? Pray, Mrs. Lonergan, what has the Catholic Church to do with his niceness? Answer me that at your leisure, Ma'am;" and he screwed up one eye, and looked hard at the widow with the other, thereby intimating that he considered the question he had propounded an unanswerable poser.

"Well, at all events, you'll admit he's a humane and charitable man?—every one allows that of him," urged the widow, determined not to be wholly silenced.

"The more's the pity it's a heretic that's in it," retorted his reverence, returning to his original objection, and leaving the poor widow, in familiar parlance, "without a leg to stand upon." Doctor O'Flynn, though a learned man, who could write with the ease and correctness of a scholar, was apt to indulge colloquially in provincialisms, and occasionally in vulgarisms also,—a habit prevalent at the time amongst educated people, but which in our day is confined almost exclusively to the unlettered classes. "I tell you, Mrs. Lonergan," he continued, "that if there's a warmer corner than another there, it will be reserved for him. Doesn't he, and the likes of him, assemble in their Lodges, which ought to be called 'Hellfire Clubs,' and denounce our Church, and revile our Holy Father the Pope, who is the light of the world? Does he not wantonly abuse us, poor Catholics, as if we had no right to live upon God's earth at all? A nice man, indeed! Oh! Mrs. Lonergan, I'm surprised at you, Ma'am."

Doctor O'Flynn was now growing warm on a subject he had been known to treat most eloquently, and there was really no conceiving when or how he would have ended, had not Catherine, with admirable ingenuity, executed a piece of strategy which effectually succeeded in soothing his reverence, and calming his ruffled feelings. Like all who sojourn in this nether sphere, Father O'Flynn had his weaknesses; whilst we are of the earth, we must be earthy; and our reverend friend was terrestrial in that he had a fancy—a *penchant*—a fondness, it may be—for the wine of Oporto, that is, real port, not the spurious compound commonly vended as such, which resembles the generous wine it imitates only in colour; for the doctor was a connoisseur, and knew what real wine was. This was the only potation he indulged in, and, to do him justice, he did so in moderation, and, like a gentleman, only in the evening, when his clerical functions were disposed of.

All this was known to Catherine, who, finding the doctor in one of his refractory humours, availed herself of her knowledge to charm away his wrath. It happened that the widow had a store of some genuine wine, the remnant of a stock selected by her late husband, which the doctor was well acquainted with,—a delicious, fine old port, that caused him who once partook of it to cherish throughout life a vivid recollection of the event. It was old, and well crusted; racy and mellow; sufficiently dry to please the most fastidious gourmand, yet fruity and rich enough to gratify the most luxurious palate. It was wine that would dispel care, and leave no sting behind. One sip of it would silence the noisiest water-drinker that ever spouted on behalf of the pump, or deluged society with whole torrents of eloquence on the virtues of toast and water. The mere aroma of it would restore warmth to the breast of a misanthrope, and force out all the wrinkles from his withered heart. What wonder, then, that it had charms for the doctor, who had known it in almost every stage of its existence; for he had drunk it fresh from the wood, when with the fire and freshness of youth it mounted to the head, and set the pulse in motion; he had tasted it, when, mellowed and matured, yet active and vigorous withal, it gave promise of more decided excellence in years to come; and now in its old age, when it had reached the very acmé of perfection, could he be unmindful of its virtues? Oh, Catherine! it was a master-stroke of thine to introduce this ambrosial wine at such a juncture. For a brief space she disappeared from the scene, leaving the widow to bear the whole weight of the doctor's wrath; but now the blooming Hebe returns, bearing a crystal vessel of the sparkling nectar, which, while apparently unconscious of the doctor's presence, she placed beside him, diffusing, as she did so, a bouquet of perfume that at once reminded the reverend gentleman of his mundane nature. As he surveyed the decanter containing the precious fluid, a glow of happiness passed over his features, and he smiled benignantly on the fair girl who had thus anticipated his wants.

"Won't you take a glass of wine, Sir, your favourite port?" asked Catherine, in a tone so insinuating, that St. Anthony could not have resisted her.

The doctor gently murmured his assent, and the daughter of Eve helped him plenteously.

His reverence heaved a gentle sigh, took a sip or two of wine, and laid down his glass, at peace with Catherine and with all the world.

Though rigid and inflexible in his principles, and a strict disciplinarian in matters of duty, Dr. O'Flynn was by no means the harsh and unyielding character he seemed: ascetic, and even stern in his aspect and discourse, he bore beneath the surface a soft and gentle heart, and a fund of true benevolence that few believed him gifted with. The early discipline he had been subjected to, with perhaps an acute sense of wrong arising from the disabilities that he and his order laboured under, had stamped their hard lines upon him; but these formed only the outer crust, or stratum, that concealed a mine of gold beneath.

As he surveyed the fair girl with the affection and tenderness of a father, he thought of the melancholy prospect that lay before her, and the pitiable consequences that would follow, if so much innocence and beauty should be sacrificed, as he believed they would, if she united herself in marriage with one over whom his Church had not only no control, but whom it branded as an outcast and a heretic. Such a union he considered the greatest affliction that could befall her; but, reluctant to pain her by again returning to the subject, he refrained from renewing the conversation. After debating within himself as to how he should act, he resolved on effecting a compromise: he would lay before her the danger of the course she was pursuing, but in a manner so kind and gentle, that she could not feel angered with him, and he doubted not that the words he should thus instil into her heart should fructify there.

"Now, Kate, my dear," said he, opening the trenches, as it were, preparatory to making his grand assault, "you know I have no selfish ends to gratify. Attend then, my child, while I bestow upon you a little friendly admonition—friendly, d'ye mind, Catherine,—which I trust will be profitable to you." Here his reverence smiled complacently upon the widow, to intimate that his wrath was appeased, and that the little feud between them was over. The lady received his advances with cheerfulness, and resumed all her wonted serenity. There was such real kindness in his manner, and so much good humour in his countenance, that Kate, whom angry tones would not have moved, sat down beside him, and listened attentively to his remarks.

"My child," he continued, "you must not be displeased, if what I am about to say should prove distasteful to you, for I am only doing my duty. I intend now, Catherine, to give you such cogent reasons for turning up this young boy,—hem,—heretic I mean, that you'll shun him as you would the plague, a mad dog, or any other unpleasantness of the kind; and, to guard against the chance of his ever enticing you into matrimony, you'll not rest content until you wed the tidy young man I have in my eye for you." At this allusion to the collector, the doctor and the widow exchanged familiar glances. "So now to begin," continued the doctor, "a-hem!" He had evidently a splendid argument to unfold, and was conscious of the fact; for he smiled complacently,—a habit peculiar to him in such felicitous moments. Carefully clearing his throat, so that every word he uttered should fall with its full force on Kate's obedient ear, he was on the point of commencing, when an unexpected and perplexing occurrence took place, and the brilliant oration was lost to the world for ever. The door at the moment flew open, and—David Elliott the Orangeman stalked in amongst them.—*He called for his umbrella.* The poor widow was not only nonplussed, but terrified. Toward men of such opposite principles, between whom such bitter cause of animosity existed, she know not how to act. At one time she expected that the doctor would open his Breviary, and proceed with the service for laying the devil, or that some other awful catastrophe must ensue. Her apprehensions, however, were entirely unfounded; for Dr. O'Flynn was a gentleman, and knew how to comport himself with proper dignity on such an occasion. As for the alderman, he resolved for the time to keep his Orangeism and loyalty in abeyance, and to act towards the great champion of Romanism with that courtesy which belligerents display towards each other on the territory of a neutral. Thus animated, he took the seat he was invited to with much suavity and self-possession, dividing his attentions between the widow, whom he regarded with a respectful homage largely tinctured with admiration, and her reverend friend, upon whom he looked with an urbanity of countenance that courted familiarity and invited conference. At first the doctor assumed rather a severe and repellant demeanour: but, softened by the conciliatory bearing of the Orangeman, he gradually relaxed; and when the latter had been helped to a glass of the excellent port before them, and pronounced a high eulogium on its merit, a community of feeling was established between them that broke down all restraint, and placed the gentlemen on easy and friendly terms. The ice that had encompassed his reverence had thawed, and his genial nature now shone forth in all its warmth. He could not have been angry now, had he tried to become so. As he leaned back in his chair, with his well-turned nether limbs in their clerical black shorts and silk stockings negligently disposed the one over the other, and his wine glass in his hand, which "ever and anon he gave his *lips*," he seemed the very impersonation of peace and tranquillity. Never had charm wrought a greater effect than that administered by Catherine. Nor was our friend Mr. Elliott less happy; so engrossed was he by the widow's charms, and so intoxicated with the love which every glance of her's inspired him with, that all his Orange zeal and partizanship remained shrouded in forgetfulness; and although in an abstract way he considered the doctor, in right of his calling, the very embodiment of evil, he was not only prepared to enter into a truce with that gentleman, but, if required, to swear eternal friendship towards him. Bye and bye Catherine discovered that there was a pack of cards at hand, when it was found that Alderman Elliott was fond of a rubber of whist, a game at which the doctor considered himself a master. They cut for partners, and the widow came to Mr. Elliott. Surely nothing could have happened luckier. Father O'Flynn, rousing himself for action, determined to let the Orangeman see that it was no common person he had to deal with; and our hero, in his turn, vowed internally he would convince his opponent that a Protestant and an Orangeman would never submit to defeat. To do justice to the alderman, it must be owned that he played admirably for the first five minutes, but then he broke down miserably; for the truth was, the sparkling eyes of the widow, in which there were whole volumes of expression eloquent with love, completely disconcerted him. Whenever he met their glance, and that was very often —for there was a fascination in them that irresistibly impelled him to gaze upon their bright effulgence— his heart, which was forty-five years old, every day of it, so beat and fluttered that all his calculations were upset, and he was sure to throw the wrong card; and then his partner chid him for his blunder, but yet so sweetly as to tempt him to err again, to bring down upon him a repetition of reproofs.

Never was Father O'Flynn known to be in better humour; his youthful partner was true to him as the needle to the pole; so skilfully did she play, that he was delighted with her conduct, and lauded her unceasingly. He was winning rapidly; and so indeed was the alderman, but in a different sense. With that prescience ever attendant upon true talent, Kate saw from the first that the day was her own, and her spirits rose in consequence to a height of exuberance rendering her vivacity personified. Taking no thought for the morrow, and giving way to a fund of wit and gaiety, yet ever attending with scientific skill to the game, she kept the company in a ferment of merriment and good humour:—never had Catherine played her cards so well.

The night imperceptibly wore round; and had not the appetites of the party, with the fidelity of a chronometer, assured them that several hours must have elapsed, they would have mistaken midnight for an early hour of the evening. This crisis had been anticipated, and amply provided for by the admirable girl we have been commending. A snow-white napkin was now dexterously spread upon the table, and an excellent supper, hot and odoriferous, placed before them. The appearance of the viands proved so opportune and grateful, that under their influence Doctor O'Flynn became quite humorous, giving utterance to several respectable old jokes and witticisms, that met with unqualified approval from the company, who indeed were in such excellent spirits as to be pleased with everything. It was wonderful to observe the intimacy, and even friendship, that had sprung up between the gentlemen. The widow was amazed at the phenomenon; and could hardly credit her senses, when she heard his reverence address the Orangeman in such terms as, "My dear Sir" and "My friend," and Elliott in his turn reciprocate these friendly terms. Yet so it was; the contact of the gentlemen had produced kindred impressions upon each—Doctor O'Flynn found, from his short acquaintance with Elliott, that he was by no means the monster of bigotry and intolerance he had been described to him; and the alderman very soon saw that O'Flynn, though the zealot, or it may be bigot, he had been represented, was withal a gentleman, with a good heart, and as much capacity for friendship as other men.

They broke up about twelve o'clock. Alderman Elliott had lost his heart, and about five-and-twenty shillings; but he had won the widow, there could be no doubt upon the subject. When the gentlemen found themselves in the street, the alderman gave his arm to his companion, and insisted on seeing him home; and when his reverence was left at his own door, and saw Mr. Elliott retracing his steps, he declared it would be an act unchristianlike in the extreme to allow him to proceed alone at so late an hour, and accordingly he returned with him. And now that they were once more in Thomas-street, Alderman Elliott expressed it as his unqualified conviction, that he would be ashamed of himself if he allowed a clergyman to traverse the streets of Dublin at that unseasonable hour without an escort, and declared that he would not part his friend until he had accompanied him back again and seen him safely housed, which after considerable difficulty he succeeded in doing; and we have no doubt that his reverence on that night enjoyed sound and undisturbed repose. It was not so, however, with Mr. Elliott; for when he retired to his couch, it was to dream of the beauteous widow,—her bewitching smile, and her pearly teeth, her soft dark eyes, and her merry laugh, and his own unaccountable stupidity in not having discovered her perfections sooner. After all, it must be conceded that sleep under such circumstances is by no means disagreeable.

CHAPTER VII.

"And while thou livest, dear Kate, take a fellow of plain and uncoined constancy, for he perforce must do thee right, because he hath not the gift to woo in other places: for these fellows of infinite tongue that can rhyme themselves into ladies' favours—they do always reason themselves out again. What! a speaker is but a prater; a rhyme is but a ballad; a good leg will fall; a straight back will stoop; a black beard will turn white; a curled pate will grow bald; a fair face will wither; a full eye will wax hollow; but a good heart, Kate, is the sun and moon; or rather the sun, and not the moon, for it shines bright, and never changes, but keeps his course truly. If thou would'st have such a one: take me. . . . . And what sayest thou then to my love? Speak! my fair, and fairly, I pray thee."

It has been seen that David Elliott was deeply smitten with the fair young widow. The fact, in truth, was that he became enamoured with her from the first moment he had seen her, although his feelings for some time did not assume a definite form. Having been engrossed the greater part of his life with the cares of business, and with his Orange Lodge and its associates, he had seen but little of female society; so that, although naturally of a domestic turn, he had been obliged by the force of circumstances to lead a life in which domestic happiness was unknown. The transition from this to the society of the lovely widow, had for him all the zest and novelty that green fields and flowers have for the jaded denizen of a city.

Although the Orange Association, of which he was so active a member, was essentially a sectarian body, whose main principle was hostility to the Roman Catholic religion, and the ascendancy in the State of Protestantism, he was not, as has before been observed, a bigot properly so called. An Orangeman, like many at the present day, more from association and habit than from principle, he was but slightly imbued with the narrow, intolerant opinions entertained by the Orange body in general; for his large and liberal heart warmed to all men as his fellow-creatures, entirely irrespective of their creed or station. Yet his generous nature had withal been so warped by the deadly influence of prejudice, that, while his heart abounded with good will towards all men, and while in the ordinary intercourse of life he knew no religious distinctions, he would at one time as soon have thought of committing suicide as of selecting for the wife of his bosom a person professing the Romish form of Christianity. Born and reared a Protestant, and brought up from childhood in Orange principles, his acquaintance with Catholics had been wholly confined to business relations; so that, knowing little of them in a domestic point of view, and influenced as he was so much by prejudice, he could not have believed it possible for a person of that religion to be educated and polished as others were; for it was the habit amongst Protestants at the time to look upon their Roman Catholic fellow-countrymen as an inferior race, incapable of lofty or generous principles, and unfit to hold any position of respectability or importance.

Previous to his introduction to Mrs. Lonergan, his distorted imagination had depicted her as a withered old duenna, all craft and subtlety, actuated by one absorbing passion,—the aggrandizement of the Roman Catholic Church by any means,—and deadly hatred to the Protestant community. But when he had seen the widow, and found her in every respect the contrary to that which in his ignorance he had conceived her; when he had found her to be a young and beautiful woman, amiable in disposition, polished in manners, and, what was more rare at the time, well educated withal, a complete reaction took place within him, and his feelings towards her and the Roman Catholic body in general underwent an entire change. He had not, as a Protestant, surrendered any of the religious principles he had been reared in; but he had, to a great extent, overmastered his religious prejudices. The fact that he had spent all his life in warfare against Romanists caused him to regard the widow with more interest than perhaps he would otherwise have displayed towards her; and by way of making atonement for the bigotry and prejudices he had indulged in, he sought to propitiate her by every means in his power, and would marry her if he could. Yet here lay a mountain of difficulty. He was a conscientious Protestant—she an equally sincere Catholic; the union of such people at the time was a thing almost unheard of. Fascinated with her, yet not knowing how to reconcile himself to the attachment, nor indeed how he could expect her to reciprocate his passion, he saw before him a host of difficulties and obstructions to be surmounted ere he could attain his object. The problem, he felt, was easy of solution, yet how to solve it he knew not. In his incertitude he found himself in a sea of perplexity; and though he saw a haven in the distance, he knew not how to steer for it. A paradise of bliss lay before him; but how to clear the intervening obstacles he knew not. And thus ran the current of his thoughts: he loved the charming widow, who in person, age, and disposition, was all that he could desire in a wife, but then—she was a Roman Catholic—*a Papist*. The recollection of this for the moment aroused all his old prejudices, but only to disappear again, as his vivid fancy conjured up before him her lovely countenance, upon which was imprinted all the sweetness and beauty of the Christian; then why, he asked himself, should he regard her with disfavour because of her religion, the tenets of which she conscientiously believed in, just as he did in those of his own? After all, what was Romanism but one form of Christianity, and Protestantism but another? Both were the same in essentials, but differing in discipline and details. What a charming companion for his lonely fireside! How dull and miserable was his home now! No lovely wife to chase away discontent and gloom—his only companions the stupid revellers he used nightly to carouse with! How besotted was the life he had been leading! The intellect that had been intrusted to him to be cultivated—so that, like a diamond wrought by the lapidary, it should shine forth in its brightness and raise him near unto the angels—neglected, despised, and trampled on; allowed "to rust in him unused." Smothered in drink!—trampled in the mire!—the intellectual gift, to him, was a pearl cast before a swine. As these convictions floated through his mind, he felt, as in his excitement he paced to and fro, that he would give all the world's goods he possessed to be able to build up a wall of brass that would effectually shut out from his memory the present and the past. But might he not retrace the path to virtue, and forget the past in the future? Yes, he would try and do so. A great living writer has said—"There is a future left to all men who have the virtue to repent, and the energy to atone;" and such a conviction, though not expressed in terms, flashed through Elliott's mind. He felt that, in the companionship of the woman he so loved—whose moral and intellectual endowments shone in her fair, expressive countenance—he could begin and lead a new life. But again came the fatal objection—she was a Roman Catholic; yet why, again he asked himself, should he allow religion to influence him in the matter? Could they not—while husband and wife, and all in this world to each other—worship their common Creator in the manner they conceived most acceptable to Him, and thus by different routes reach the same goal at last, and ultimately meet together in heaven? And then he thought of his son—his only child—whom he had begun of late to regard with pride and renewed affection; and of the fond and trusting girl upon whom he had placed his affections, the daughter of the woman he loved so well. What happiness was in store for all, if he could only see his way out of the wood! But, then, what would be said of him by those with whom he had associated all his life, if he deserted the principles he had so long professed, and allied himself with Roman Catholics? Hatred, contempt, and derision awaited him; the brand of a renegade and traitor would be placed upon him. Deserted and derided by his friends, he felt he would be a wretched and forsaken man. Yet, no,—not forsaken; for with the woman he loved, how could he feel alone in the world? Still he quailed at the vista thus opened to his view, and became involved in a labyrinth of doubts, fears, and perplexities; through which, however, there flitted before him, even in the darkest and most intricate moments, the vision of the lovely widow, which seemed to encourage him to proceed, and to guide him onward through the devious maze; for it never occurred to him that she would refuse him. It was not vanity that led him to think so; but because she had afforded him reason to believe she returned his love. Without overstepping the bounds of the strictest delicacy and decorum, she had given him so much encouragement to persevere in his addresses, that he could not believe she meant to trifle with him. No; she was too good, too kind, to encourage hopes she did not mean to realize. Thus it was that "he laid the flattering unction to his soul," that he was not indifferent to her. The difficulties he had at first encountered were now rapidly clearing away, and he was beginning to see the way before him. His mind at length was made up; he would propose; and, if accepted, would marry her in the face of all the world. Why should he be ashamed to do that which was honest, lawful, and right? Filled with this determination, he communicated his intentions to his son—to whom it was a labour of love, in its true sense, to approve of and commend the course his father had resolved on. So eloquently did he discourse on the happy prospects before them, and in so sensible a light did he place all matters connected with it, that David Elliott marched off boldly to the widow, determined to carry off the prize despite of all opposition.

But let us see what were the lady's feelings respecting our hero. From her first interview with him, she had looked upon him with favour; for there was that in his appearance which, while externally marking the gentleman, is characteristic of an innate gentleness and nobility that wins its way with every one. Though not a young man, he was in the prime of life, and was what most women would consider a handsome, fine-looking man. Aware of all this, and conscious also that he regarded her with a homage and admiration too real to be simulated, which no woman is ever insensible to, it was not surprising that she favoured his advances. With such partiality, indeed, did she regard him, that by the time their first meeting was over, the work of courtship was more than half accomplished. There was, however, a further motive which actuated her in this respect: gifted as she was with personal attractions that alone would have caused her to be eagerly sought for as a wife, she was endowed with golden ones also to a considerable extent, that rendered her a double prize to all wife-seekers to whom money was an object. Her late husband, who had been a man of excellent character, and not at all such as old Mr. Coates had represented him, having in the course of a long life of honest industry realized considerable property, had left her amply provided for. In consequence of this, the widow had from time to time had many suitors, all of whom she had received indifferently, or discarded, mainly from a belief that they were influenced in their addresses by pecuniary considerations. Disgusted at length at the sordid motives, as she conceived, of her suitors, she became morbidly sensitive on the subject, and, unmindful of her personal attractions, regarded every man who looked upon her with admiration as an adventurer or fortune-hunter. So impressed had she become with this feeling, that she had vowed at one time never again to enter into the married state. When, however, our hero made his advances, all these misgivings vanished; for his own ample means and his character as a merchant and public man placed him entirely beyond any unworthy imputations of the kind, and served as a guarantee for the honour and probity of his intentions. Pleased that she had at length met with a suitor who valued her for herself alone, she would have accepted him at once without any hesitation, but for one serious objection—he was a *Protestant*. She had been taught from childhood to hold extreme opinions on religious subjects, and to regard Protestantism not only as a heresy, but as a form of worship worse than Heathenism, inasmuch as the ignorant and uninformed Heathen follows his religion from ignorance of a better one, while Protestants, as her instructors taught her, obstinately persisted in their unbelief, although the true Church held its lantern before them, pointing out the path that leads to everlasting life. How could a Catholic, the near relation of a bishop, having a host of minor ecclesiastics her relations and friends, commit such an error as marry not only a Protestant, but one whose whole life had been marked by his hostility to Romanism,—who was, as her friend Doctor O'Flynn had characterized him, "a rank Orangeman?" Her reason, moulded on the religious tenets she had been reared in, taught her that it would be dangerous and wrong to intermarry with such a man; but the dictates of her heart and of her own clear judgment, unbiassed by sectarian views, assured her that she would be right and blameless in accepting him for her husband. For the widow, like our hero, had no real bigotry whatever. She followed in sincerity and truth the religion she had been reared in; she loved and honoured God as the source of all good,—the Author and Giver of all that this bright world affords; and, like every real Christian, was humble and tolerant,—more ready to persuade by the force of example, than by the means resorted to by modern zealots for making converts to their views. In her feelings towards Mr. Elliott she was warmly supported by her daughter, who constantly importuned her to dismiss all scruples from her mind, and to favour his suit; for the young girl held the alderman in that respect and esteem with which people generally regard those whom they consider immeasurably their superiors, and with anxious heart she looked forward to the day when he and her mother should be united; and with all the ardour of youth, she saw a bright world of bliss before her when she should become young Elliott's wife, and they should all form one happy family group. The realization of this pleasing picture, however easy of accomplishment it appeared to the daughter, was looked upon by the mother almost as an impossibility. In fact, when she contemplated the position of affairs, she became involved in quite as much perplexity as Mr. Elliott had found himself placed in. She saw happiness for her daughter and herself in the proposed union; but the cup of joy, though overflowing, was seasoned with bitters. Her inclinations all pointed one way; but duty to herself and family, as she considered, tended to the other: wide was the chasm that should be passed before the desired goal could be reached.

While she was in this state of indecision our hero arrived upon the scene flushed with ardour, and determined to secure the rich prize he sought for. Both parties had passed the age of sentimentalism; so there is but little to record as to the mode in which our friend made his overtures, inasmuch as he came at once to the mark like a man, assuring the fair widow that from the moment he had first seen her she had won his admiration and regard; and that every hour that had since passed had confirmed his first impressions, until his feelings towards her had ripened into the most enduring love. The widow, who heard his statement with evident pleasure, candidly owned that he was nct indifferent to her; and that were she to consult her own feelings she would not hesitate in accepting his proposals, the more so, as in doing so she would gratify the wishes and promote the happiness of her daughter; but that, differing so much as they did in religion, she felt she could not accept him as a husband, her family being all zealous Catholics, who looked upon him as a foe to themselves and to all they held most dear, inasmuch as he and his family had been always distinguished for hostility to the religion they professed. The substance of this speech, which the widow delivered with an ease and grace of manner truly feminine, only served to stimulate her suitor to persevere more strongly; and now David Elliott delivered an harangue, the eloquence and impetuosity of which quite astonished the lady. In the course of it he showed her that in a religious point of view neither should object to the other; that common Christianity united them both, although they differed in their modes of professing it; that religion, rightly understood, consisted not in the rigid adherence to the tenets of this or that peculiar sect, but in loving and serving God with one's whole heart, and acting towards our fellow-men as we would wish they should act towards us. "I shall never," said he in conclusion, "attempt to interfere with you in the exercise of your religion; for I do not believe that it tends to the true worship of God to unsettle the religious convictions of any Christian after they have been once definitely formed: we shall each follow the form of worship we have been reared in, and be the better Christians for doing so: thus by following sincerely the religion you have been reared in you shall please me rather than otherwise. As for me," said he, "I shall prove myself so fond a husband, so sincere a Protestant, and in consequence so much a better man and Christian than I have been, as to prove more effectually than by a whole volume of sermons the truth of the statements I have advanced; and as for yourself, you shall serve God so devoutly, and prove such a sweet and loving wife as to convince me that a Catholic may not only be a Christian, but an angel. Then take me for your husband, and come and cheer my lonely house, and fill my heart with gladness. I know I am neither good nor young enough for you; but if you will enrich me with your love, to atone for my deficiencies and short comings, I promise you that the remainder of my life shall be one uninterrupted course of devoted affection. You shall be the delight of my eyes; the joy of my heart; my pearl; my pride, my consolation. And, taking her tiny hand in his, which she sought not to withdraw, he continued—"Come, what say you now? won't you have me? Kill me not with a dreadful—no;" and he looked into the face of the blushing widow, who betrayed such bewitching confusion as threw the middle-aged gentleman into an ecstasy of delight.

"I know not what to say," she replied, evidently yielding to his importunities—"if I accept you, all my friends will condemn me."

"My dearest love," said Elliott, "is not this a matter that concerns you and me more than any friend?

If by our marriage we secure each other's happiness, why should we hesitate because our friends may object?"

"But what would be thought of me if I accepted you without consulting a single relation except my daughter, who is little more than a child in years? There's my cousin, the bishop, I should acquaint him; and I could not avoid consulting Dr. O——"

This was the critical moment: the alderman knew that "O'Flynn" was coming; and however much he esteemed that reverend gentleman, he did not think it at all advisable to consult him on the occasion.

"I tell you what you'll do," said he, before she had time to pronounce the name—"marry me first, and consult him afterwards; that's the course I mean to follow with *my* friends—they who try to please every one generally end by pleasing nobody. Let us only consult our own hearts in the first instance, and begin by pleasing ourselves; and you'll find that, having done so, all our friends in a very short time will become well pleased also."

The wisdom of the course thus pointed out was so manifest, that the widow, like a sensible woman, yielded to it at once. He saw acquiescence in her eyes, which beamed upon him a full soul of love; he felt it in the gentle pressure of her hand; and so elated did he become, that, unmindful of her blushes, which indeed only served to inflame him the more, he clasped the lovely widow in his arms, like an old fool as he was, and gave her some dozen kisses, and thus the marriage contract was sealed.

CHAPTER VIII.

"I have long dreamed of such a kind of man,
So surfeit-swelled, so old, and so profane,
But being awake I do despise my dream;
Make less thy body hence, and more thy grace;
Leave gormandizing: know the grave doth gape
For thee thrice wider than for other men—
Reply not to me with a fool-born jest;
Presume not that I am the thing I was;
For Heaven doth know, so shall the world perceive,
That I have turned away my former self:
So will I those that kept me company."

Alderman Elliott, it has been seen, absented himself from "the Lodge" upon two successive evenings—an enormity that filled Brother Coates with so much alarm, that the old gentleman, all disquietude and apprehension, called upon his kinsman to learn the cause of his absence. The cunning old fox, to impart solemnity and importance to his visit, led the alderman to believe that he was delegated by the members of the Lodge to obtain a formal explanation of his conduct. "Brother Elliott, why were you absent from the Lodge on our two last meetings?" demanded the old fellow, with a sternness and authority becoming a grand Inquisitor—"I ask you the question, as I shall be obliged to report your answer to the brethren to-morrow."

"My dear Bob, I have not been at all the same man I was for some time past," returned the alderman, in a subdued and mournful tone, such as would proceed from an invalid who had learned for the first time that he laboured under a mortal disease which no human skill could alleviate; "I have been labouring under an affection which I did my best to combat against, but to which I have been obliged at last to succumb; I'm not right here, Bob, that's the fact;" and, pressing his hand over the region of his heart, he looked dolefully in his friend's face, yet with a sly twinkle in his eye, and a twittering round the corners of his mouth, that imparted a comic expression to his countenance, altogether at variance with his statement.

"God bless us! you don't mean to say you've got disease of the heart?" exclaimed Bob Coates, jumping from his seat, quite aghast, while he surveyed his afflicted friend with the most anxious concern.

"I'm afraid it's too true, Bob," returned the alderman, with difficulty preserving his gravity; for the expression of anxiety and alarm on poor old Coates's withered and besotted countenance was ludicrous in the extreme.

"My poor dear fellow, how I feel for you!" continued Bob Coates, with the utmost sympathy and condolence. "I'm told there's no complaint so treacherous as these diseases of the heart."

"None, Bob," returned the alderman, with energy; "and they always come so unexpectedly, and when they do come, 'tis so difficult to shake them off."

"It's impossible to do so, David," returned Coates—then, fearing to alarm his friend, he added, "that is, when the disease has once obtained a firm hold of you."

"There's the worst of it, Bob," broke in the alderman; "in my case I'm afraid I've encouraged the malady, so as to allow it to overmaster me. It's chronic, Bob,—it's chronic;" and, again pressing his hand to his bosom, he groaned audibly, to his old friend's evident alarm.

"Davy, my boy, we must look to this at once—we must rouse ourselves; we'll call in the first physicians of the day. Doctors have been known to effect wonders before now."

"I've no faith at all in doctors," returned the alderman, in sepulchral tones—"the malady that I am afflicted with is entirely beyond their control."

"Oh, now don't say so," returned old Coates, rising from his seat, and pacing the room in the greatest trepidation and alarm. "Terrible news this will be to the brethren! terrible news! we little thought when we missed you at the festive board last night, that your valuable life was in danger—oh dear! oh dear!" And, quite overcome, he threw himself into a seat, and either feeling or affecting a sudden weakness, he begged of his kinsman to administer a stimulant.—"The cowld perspiration's on my forehead," said he, "and I've a wakeness down the small of my back; and if you'd just let me have a drain of something warm, you'd revive me; for raly I want the like after the startling intelligence you've conveyed to me."

Alarmed for his old friend, Elliott promptly produced a flask of brandy, and, pouring out a glassful, was about to dilute it with water, when old Coates, observing the movement, murmured gently, "Nate this time, David,—nate—'twill bring me round the speedier;" and in obedience to the request his friend handed him a supply of the ardent spirit, which the old fellow despatched with the ease that an infant swallows new milk.

"That will do, David,—bless you—I'm quite myself now," he returned, brightening up; "the French are a wonderful people surely, I mean in regard of the drop o' the drink, for their brandy is beautiful. But to return to yourself, David—what's to be done at all? that's what I want to know."

"I only know of one remedy, Bob," returned the alderman, with the same droll expression on his face that has before been remarked, "and that I'm resolved to try; it's a serious one, Bob—for when you once venture upon it, you must continue it all your life, whether it agrees with you or not."

"What is it, Davy my boy? what is it?" asked Coates.

"It's a receipt of my own; and, kill or cure, I intend to venture upon it," was the alderman's response.

"Don't resort to quackery, David, for thousands have been killed by it," argued Bob Coates; "there's that rascal O'Rafferty Macan killing people by hundreds with his nostrums, yet making a fortune by his villiany, and calling himself a philanthropist at the same time—avoid him, David, as you would the plague."

"Never fear, Bob," returned Elliott, laughing heartily, in spite of himself; "I don't mean to patronize any of Professor Macan's fraternity, or their nostrums."

"But what is it, David? what is it, my boy?" urged Coates, all curiosity and impatience.

"I'm afraid, Bob, you'd consider the remedy so dangerous, that you'd disapprove of it altogether; so you must excuse me for not disclosing it at present. Of this, however, you may be assured, that it is not so very formidable after all; for I've known many others in exactly the same condition as myself who have tried it with the greatest success. In fact, Bob, I'm so sanguine on the subject as to consider it a complete cure."

"Well, that is very consolatory," returned old Coates; "and you raly think the recipe you spake of will prove serviceable to you."

"Think, Bob! I'm sure of it."

"Well raly I'm delighted at all this, yes; de—lighted," returned Mr. Coates; "aye, and so will Debby be when she hears the news; that is, she'll be happy to find you're not in danger of your life." The lady alluded to as Debby was Mr. Coates's daughter, whom he had designed for young Elliott's partner.

"Ah! by-the-bye, Bob, how is Deborah?" asked the alderman, reminded of that young lady by Bob Coates's allusion; "you mentioned some time back that she was poorly."

"And so she is still," returned Coates, in a confidential tone—"she's pining away, David, she's pining; but it couldn't be otherwise: however, it's no matter, no matter in life," and he heaved a sigh, and affected to brush away a tear.

"Bless my soul! has anything happened?" asked Elliott, with some alarm.

"Oh, don't mind, David, don't concern yourself at all about it," continued Coates; "you see she is such an affectionate creature, and takes things so much to heart, and all too for the sake of others. Would you believe now, she has been crying the very eyes out of her head since she heard of that unfortunate affair of William Nassau's? you can't at all fancy how she has suffered on his account."

"Oh, has she?" observed the alderman, drily.

"Her sufferings have been acute and painful," continued Coates, unheeding the remark; "I never saw anything like it; but it's only natural, for she positively adores William Nassau—no sister ever loved a brother like it: do you know what she said to me the other evening?"

"No, Bob, let's have it."

"She had just asked me what kind of person this young famale was. 'My dear, I can't tell you,' said I; 'all I know respecting her is, that she is a Papist, and that all belonging to her are so too.' 'Is she good-looking?' asked Debby. 'I can't tell you, child,' says I. 'Well, I know what I'll do,' said she; 'I'll watch for the woman until I see her in her mother's shop, and I'll then go in and make some trifling purchase to enable me to get a proper view of her. Yes, I'll contrive to see her, though I perish in the attempt.' And positively and actually the dear girl cleverly and courageously went through the undertaking, and succeeded bravely. Oh, Debby's a good girl—a very good girl indeed, and the man who marries her will be blessed."

"And what did Deborah think of Miss Lonergan?" asked the alderman, who had his own opinion on the subject.

"Now, here is the aggravating part of it," returned Bob Coates, with the air of an injured man. "What was Debby's answer, when I put to her the very question you have just asked? 'She's a fright,' said she—'a horrid rowdy'—no, I'm wrong, she said a dowdy—'a horrid dowdy, with great staring black eyes, an unnatural long nose, and false ringlets—a nasty, ugly, forward creature; and I hate her;' and she burst into tears, and the dear girl has never had a dry eye since. Now this, I say, makes matters doubly provoking," wound up old Coates, and he turned to his friend for sympathy, but only to be miserably disappointed; for the old gentleman's story was so absurd, while the voice and gesture with which it was delivered was so provocative of fun, that our hero, notwithstanding his natural kindness of heart, was unable to restrain himself from breaking into successive fits of laughter, which were all the more violent from his efforts to suppress them.

Unable to understand the cause of this, old Coates surveyed his kinsman with a perplexed and bewildered air, that was perfectly ludicrous; but, finding that his companion's mirth was rather increasing than abating, his temper failed him, and he rose from his seat, looking fiercely around. "I don't understand what all this means," said he; "I'm not aware of having given cause for this hilarity—I did'nt come here to be insulted," and he buttoned up his coat, and looked round for his hat. The alderman, who possessed a large fund of good nature, now promptly apologized, assuring his friend that he was surprised to think his son could fall in love with so plain a person as Miss Lonergan was described.

"Yes, that's just the view we took of it," continued old Coates, whose wrath was at once appeased. "'If she was good-looking,' said Debby, 'I could forgive William Nassau; but as it is, oh, it's horrid!' and she again gave way to tears, and the dear girl has never had a dry eye since."

"Well, Bob, we must try and get William Nassau to make his peace with Deborah," returned the alderman; "meantime give her this, with my love;" and, taking from his pocket book what seemed a roll of soiled and crumpled paper, he pressed it into his kinsman's hand, and as that gentleman promptly accepted the gift by clasping it lovingly, causing it to crisp as only fine tissue paper does, and then treasured it up carefully in his pocket, and afterwards warmly pressed the donor's hand, we are irresistibly drawn to infer that what had been thus confided to Mr. Coates for his daughter's use was a sheaf of bank notes, a commodity which is welcome to every one, however soiled, greasy, or unclean.

This timely present restored Bob Coates to his wonted cheerfulness; for the old gentleman laboured under a chronic complaint, very prevalent in all ages, known as scarcity of cash, to which his friend's generosity promised to afford considerable relief. And now Mr. Coates, having been provided with "materials," drank and chatted away until an exceedingly late hour indeed. In short, he made another night of it—we use the singular pronoun, for Alderman Elliott scarcely tasted the alcoholic fluid, although to keep his friend in company he affected to do so; and we feel bound to say, that, although upon this occasion the punch was not brewed with water from the Boyne, old Mr. Coates did it quite as much justice as if that historic river had contributed to its production. Time flew by, and the gentlemen were about to separate, when it occurred to Bob Coates to remind his friend of the banquet he had promised to regale the brethren with. "I mentioned it to some of our friends the other night," said he, "and they were delighted at the very thought; they look forward to it, I can tell you, with the greatest anxiety."

"Suppose we name the day," said the alderman; "what would you say to Monday week?"

"The deuce a better!" returned Bob Coates, in high glee.

"Good,—Monday week we'll have it. I can't accommodate more than twenty, so I'll leave the selection to you."

"Never fear me, David," returned Bob Coates, in a high state of delight; "I'll choose the staunchest and jolliest of the lot; we'll come in full canonicals—every man shall have on his blue coat and Orange scarf."

"Bravo, Bob! ever true blue," returned the alderman, laughing heartily.

This important point having been settled, Bob Coates fortified himself with another bumper, and rose to depart. "Good-bye, David, my boy, God bless you!" said the old fellow, wringing his friend's hand. Then, as the thought flashed upon his mind, he asked him had he called upon the Widow Lonergan, as he had advised him.

"Yes, Bob, I saw the lady, and had a long interview with her, just as you suggested," added the alderman.

"And settled everything, I hope," said Coates, with a face brimful of anxiety, though red and swollen with his potations.

"Yes, Bob, and settled everything to my entire satisfaction," returned Elliott, with a sly twinkle in his eye, and a leer upon his face, that said as plain as language could express it—"You're sold, Bob, and that too upon remarkably easy terms."

"You're a good boy, Davy, a very good boy, and I'm rayly delighted with you; for 'twould be a sarious thing if a Papist got admission into the family."

"No doubt of it, Bob," rejoined the alderman.

"And particularly as there are so many beautiful young famales of his own persuasion to be met with," added Coates, thinking of the fair Deborah at home.

"Right again, Bob, quite right!" remarked the alderman.

"Ay, ay, Davy, I'm always right: 'twas I that told you to call upon the widow—nothing like daling with principals. Now look out for some respectable young famale, and marry William Nassau off hand to her. If I were you, I would not delay an hour. Good night,—(hiccup)." And, happy as he supposed in his renewed prospects of seeing the two branches of the family, the poor and the rich, united, the old fellow trudged homeward, his nose, fiery red as it was with drink, acting as a lantern to light him on his way.

CHAPTER IX.

"Shall I ask the brave soldier who fights by my side
In the cause of mankind, if our creeds agree?
Shall I give up the friend I have valued and tried,
If he kneel not before the same altar as me?
From the heretic girl of my soul shall I fly,
To seek somewhere else a more orthodox kiss?
No! perish the heart and the laws that would try
Truth, valour, or love, by a standard like this!"

The day selected for the banquet having arrived, precisely at six o'clock in the evening some half dozen vehicles drove up to the door of Alderman Elliott's hospitable abode; and the brethren who had arrived sought admittance, dressed in their regulation costume of blue coats and white gloves, looking like so many policemen out for a holiday. Their host received them dressed rather gayer than usual, being arrayed in a bright claret-coloured coat—a fashionable garment at the time; and, by way of accounting for the splendour of his apparel, assured them that he had been at a wedding in the morning, and had not had time to exchange his clothes since. The brethren, satisfied with the statement, proceeded to administer to him the Orangeman's salute,—a piece of legerdemain which they are fond of indulging in on great occasions, and which, to let the reader into a secret, consists in applying the point of the thumb of the right hand to the top of the nose, elongating the fingers, and waving them gently to and fro; and, immediately on the signal being answered by a like movement on the part of the person saluted, grasping with the little finger of the right hand the other's corresponding finger, and shaking it heartily. By this means, absurd as it may seem, the bond of brotherhood is established between Orangemen all over the world. This important ceremony concluded, the brethren, as may be expected, grew warm and enthusiastic; and Bob Coates, who acted as leader on the occasion, unable to restrain the exuberance of his spirits, lustily exclaimed, "Hooray! who's afraid? We're all on Protestant ground now. *Here's the Pope in the pillory, and the devil pelting him with priests!*" He would have followed up this little sally by further demonstrations, when a savoury odour, ascending from the lower regions, began to float around them, occasioning a dizziness in the head, and a yearning and weakness in the gastronomic region, that entirely diverted his thoughts. The fact was, that Alderman Elliott had made his calculations to a nicety. Dinner was ready to the moment; and the brethren, downright hungry, were eager to attack it; for, knowing they would meet with plenty of good cheer at the alderman's table, they came prepared, like sensible men, to do it ample justice. As they had entered, and the hall door was closed, their tympanums were saluted with soft music, descending from an upper apartment;

and Bob Coates, hearing the sounds and taking it for granted that they breathed of "loyalty," exclaimed, in a transport of delight,—"Hooray! there's 'the first of July,' and no mistake."

"It's 'Haste to the wedding,' if it's anything," remarked another, better learned in the science of sweet sounds.

Rody Cormack now appeared, with a broad grin upon his ample visage, and with nods, winks, and gestures the most varied and grotesque, informed his master "that dinner was sarved."

"Come on, gentlemen," said the alderman, hospitably leading the way.

"Wait until we robe ourselves," returned Coates, pursing up his mouth, and assuming an air of the utmost importance, while he proceeded to array himself in an old rusty scarf that had once been orange, but was now, from old age and servitude, a dull whitey brown, relieved by a few streaks of dirty yellow—an example which the rest of the brethren followed, for on all such occasions Coates acted as their fugleman.

The procession now advanced, Bob Coates marching as stately as a drum-major at its head. Roderick, who had preceded them, threw open the parlour door, and their leader entered, closely followed by his companions in double file, like a column of infantry advancing to the assault. Bob Coates had hardly entered, when, wheeling suddenly round, he exclaimed, with consternation in his face, while he endeavoured to drive back his companions,

"May I never wet my lips with King Billy's cordial, if Father O'Flynn the priest isn't in possession,—the alderman has sold us all nately!"

This speech was quite lost on the younger members forming the rere of the procession, who, impatient at the delay, pushed forward those before them, one of them crying out,

"Go ahead there, Bob! you know we're all sharp set."

The impetus thus given drove old Mr. Coates backward, who, staggering a few paces, fell towards the corner of the room, where for a time he lay unnoticed, with his head comfortably propped up against the wall.

And now the brethren, who had all entered, became aware of the terrible deception that had been practised on them, and horror and alarm were depicted in their countenances; for there was Father O'Flynn, the Popish priest, already seated at table, apparently regardless of their presence, trying with a coolness that astounded them, the temper of a carving knife upon his thumb; while with an earnestness partaking of sternness he fixed his gaze upon a cover before him, from which a savoury odour ascended, and toyed and coquetted with his nose. The stupefied and bewildered air of the Orangemen,— the absurdity of their confusion, and their grotesque and awkward efforts to divest themselves of their yellow scarfs,—would have provoked laughter from an undertaker; for, zealots and enthusiasts as they were, they had too much right feeling to offend at such a moment the susceptibilities of his reverence. The latter saw their embarrassment; and it was only by frowning violently at the dish before him, and keeping down his risibility by repeated coughs such as would proceed from a person in the last stage of quinsey, that he was able to restrain himself from breaking into peals of laughter.

But there was another person seated at the table, *vis a vis* to the doctor, at sight of whom their astonishment was increased tenfold; for he was none other than the great Protestant champion, the Rev. Boanerges Whackimwell, the rector of the parish, and chaplain-general to the Orange Society—the greatest controversialist of the day; a divine of such extraordinary powers that he had been known to prove to the entire satisfaction of his congregation, that the Pope was Antichrist—the earthly representative of the Prince of Darkness—and that the Roman Catholic clergy were his satellites, who revolved around him, receiving and diffusing his wickedness, as the moons of Jupiter receive and reflect that luminary's effulgence; that this world was to end on the Feast of St. Michael the Archangel, better known to ordinary people as "Michaelmas Day," which was to be in the year 1864, when the Orangemen were to reign supreme over Ireland for a thousand years. A famous and remarkable man was Boanerges Whackimwell; though we are not aware of any benefit having resulted from his ministrations, or that his parishioners were rendered better Christians by the astounding discoveries he had unfolded to them.

But let us return to the brethren. For some moments

they stood confounded and perplexed, not knowing how to act; for, as they had never contemplated being placed in such a position, they were totally unprepared to meet it. Seeing no alternative but flight, they made a rush to the door: but here their retreat was prevented, for that aperture was occupied by their host and an elegant female, radiant with beauty, leaning upon his arm, whom the alderman introduced to them as his wife. The mystery was now unfolded; it was his own wedding he had attended. Great was the surprise of the brethren, who, as in duty bound, courteously saluted the lady, and heartily congratulated their friend. What the amazement and chagrin of Mr. Coates was, the reader can readily imagine, when he found that Mrs. Alderman Elliott was the quondam Widow Lonergan, the very person whom he had strenuously advised his friend to become acquainted with. Though stunned by his fall, the old fellow recovered himself in a moment, and, opening his eyes, took in at a glance the whole state of affairs. For a while he felt puzzled as to how he should act, for his position was most embarrassing. How could he congratulate his friend on his marriage with a woman whose family he had so often denounced, and with what grace could he salute the lady herself? To retire sullenly, and fall out with his friend, would be both unwise and unprofitable; yet how could he remain in such company? While still lying propped up in the corner, he debated all these points in his mind, and at length arrived at the conclusion that, under all the circumstances, the best thing he could do was to faint, which he did most artistically, keeping all the time, however, one eye partially open, and carefully noting all that was occurring before him. The bustle and confusion consequent on the meeting that had taken place having subsided, the attention of the company was attracted to the old toper, lying in the corner like a weasel asleep.

"Why, bless my soul! poor Bob has been hurt," exclaimed Mr. Elliott, observing for the first time the position of his friend.

Here Bob Coates allowed a moan of anguish to escape from him, which greatly alarmed all the company, save young Elliott, who had a strong suspicion of the real state of the case.

"Dear me! the poor man has fainted," exclaimed the lovely ex-widow, as, kneeling down, she raised the pretended sufferer's head; and chafed his temples.

"Send for a doctor!" cried Elliott, in great alarm.

"Bring sal volatile!" said another.

"Give him air and plenty of cold water!" cried others.

"None of these will serve him at all," said young Elliott; "it's brandy he wants;" and, suiting the action to the word, he applied a glassful of the fluid to the old fellow's mouth, which, notwithstanding his insensible condition, he swallowed quite wonderfully. He now revived so rapidly, that in a few minutes he was on his legs, apparently in his usual health. During the time he had lain in the pretended faint, he had brought philosophy to his aid, and had determined to put a cheerful aspect on affairs as they stood, bitter and unpalatable as they were, and to endure all with courage and fortitude. In fact, he saw there was no use whatever in acting otherwise, for it could serve no purpose; besides, there was a capital dinner awaiting them, and a range of decanters on the sideboard, affording abundant promise of an ample "jollification" afterwards. So, affecting the most unbounded astonishment at the marriage of his friend, and assuming a cheerfulness of demeanour quite wondrous under the circumstances, he wrung his kinsman's hand with a great display of cordiality, and congratulated him and his lady heartily. And now that William Nassau came forward, and introduced as his wife our merry friend Kate, the old gentleman smothered all his disappointment, and congratulated them quite as heartily as he had already done his father and his blooming partner.

The rest of the brethren, taking their cue from Bob Coates, followed his example, and all were introduced to Father O'Flynn, who shook hands with them most graciously. As for the Rev. Boanerges Whackimwell, who was their friend and chaplain, he met them like a brother. The brethren, in truth, only wanted a decent excuse for holding their ground; for, as has been observed, they were hungry, and wanted their dinners sadly.

Mrs. Alderman Elliott now entreated the gentlemen to be seated, an invitation they did not attempt to resist. They received a genuine Irish welcome, backed by excellent Irish cheer, which no mortal, be he priest, layman, or philosopher—under the pressure from within of a sharp appetite—has been ever known to resist.

All had now taken their seats at the board in the very height of good humour, and with good reason, for a more excellent dinner was never set before famished mortals. There were none of your nonsensical trifles, like painted air bubbles that collapse in a moment, having nothing but their fashionable French names to recommend them,—material falsehoods, that "hold the word of promise to the *eye*, but break it to the sense," for which our modern hospitality is sometimes remarkable,—but there was solid substantial good cheer, and plenty of it. It was not only literally, but actually, an alderman's banquet. Before Dr. O'Flynn was a haunch of venison, of the right fumette and flavour, roasted to a turn, a perfect picture in its way, with which his reverence felt perfectly at home. The alderman himself took charge of a jovial brown sirloin, the very sight of which would throw John Bull into ecstacies. To the Rev. Mr. Whackimwell was appropriated a boiled leg of mutton and trimmings, with which, from his manner of commencing operations, it was quite plain he knew well how to deal. Mr. William Nassau Elliott took upon himself the responsibility of disposing of a roast goose, a plump, jolly fellow, that crisped and fizzed and sung upon the dish, seeming to exult in each incision of the knife, and to defy him on to further efforts; like that famous but apocryphal hog, familiar to juvenile minds, that, well browned and roasted, is said to have cantered pleasantly through the streets with a knife and fork in its side, demanding of the populace to "cut and come again." The alderman's lady, who never looked better, no, not even in her days of girlhood, with the utmost affability presided over a boiled turkey, in whose demolition she proved herself an adept. It was delightful to the famished observer to mark the skill and rapidity with which she dismembered it, and left it a shapeless trunk, the mere wreck of its former self. Old Bob Coates sat opposite to a ham, to which he had taken a loving fancy, being a gem in its way; having borne the well-known Limerick brand on its obverse. It rapidly disappeared beneath the unsparing hand of our jolly old friend, who, fond of pickled meats himself (owing probably to his experience of their efficacy in promoting an appetite for the bottle), took pleasure in dispensing it around. These were the lions of the feast; but there was a host of excellent minor dishes, too numerous to particularize, to which it is only fair some allusion should be made. The fluids were not neglected; let it not for a moment be thought so. Port and sherry, Champagne and Burgundy, and ripe, racy Madeira, then a wine in general use, flowed like small beer; those who preferred it, and there were many who did so, had our own famous Dublin stout, which even in those days had attained celebrity, and justly so, for it is well deserving of patronage, and is as superior to the washy French wines now becoming fashionable, as the sirloin of beef adverted to is to a fricassee of frogs. The Rev. Boanerges Whackimwell said grace, and Doctor O'Flynn returned thanks, and indeed he had every right to do so, for he never made a more satisfactory repast in his life, albeit he was surrounded by heretics of the most virulent stamp, —an Israelite, as it were, amongst the Philistines, whose land, however, experience showed him, flowed with milk and honey.

As the cloth was removed, abundance of that liquid which Bob Coates in his facetious moments, by way of avoiding monotony, used by no means inappropriately to term "calamity water," was produced; brandy, rum, and the renowned "parliament;" and a more jovial or agreeable party, perhaps, had never met together.

When the healths of the respective brides and bridegrooms had been drunk, Bob Coates stood up, and, unmindful of all his "loyalty," proposed the health of no less a personage than Father O'Flynn,—a toast which, we feel pleasure in recording, was drunk by the Orangemen with even more than usual honours; for, not contenting themselves with drinking it in a bumper, they insisted upon paying him a symbolical tribute, pregnant with kindly feeling, which they rarely bestow upon any one save a "grand master" or "warden," at the least, and technically known amongst the brethren as "heart, pocket, and hand,"—a sort of freemasonry, which they performed by striking the palm of the right hand alternately over the region of the heart, the breeches' pocket, and the palm of the left hand, to the time "one, two, three,"—thereby signifying that their hearts, hands, and pockets were at the service of his reverence. The doctor received the compliment with much good feeling, and returned thanks in a speech of long duration, which he concluded by proposing the health of the Rev.

Mr. Whackimwell, whom he referred to as "his fellow-labourer in the vineyard,"—an allusion which Rody Cormick sagaciously informed his fellow-domestics had reference to the *wine* the reverend gentlemen were mutually indulging in.

And now William Nassau Gustavus Adolphus was upon his legs, and the company became all anxiety to hear his toast. "I give you," said he, "the memory of a king who bore a distinguished part in one of the most eventful struggles that has ever convulsed these countries."

Here old Coates imparted his apprehensions to one of the brethren in a whisper, that the speaker was about to disturb the harmony, by asking them to drink the health of "dirty King Shamus, who ran from the Boyne," as he used to designate King James the Second.

"Many of the friends I see around me," continued young Elliott, "will, I am assured, receive it with affection and respect; for the prince whose memory I propose to pay a tribute to is King William the Third."

"Bravo! Bill, bravo!" screamed Bob Coates, perfectly wild with astonishment and delight.

"In doing so," continued the speaker, unheeding Coates's interruption, "I do not characterize him merely as a successful adventurer, who hurled one despot from his throne, to make room for a greater one; who put down one species of ascendancy, to set up another in its stead; who, while he struck the fetters from one section of the people, riveted them more firmly upon another. I do not characterize him as a bigot, who denied to other men that liberty of conscience which he claimed for himself; nor do I name him as the champion of a party, or the leader of a faction—for those who have so misrepresented him belie the man, and traduce his memory. No, Gentlemen,—the great man, whose memory I ask you to honour, has higher claims upon posterity. King William was neither a tyrant nor a bigot, but a large and liberal-minded ruler, who fought, not merely for ambition, but for the benefit of mankind; a bright meteor, who arose at a time when despotism was rampant throughout the world, and dispelled for ever the moral darkness that enveloped it; who fanned the flickering embers of liberty until they burst into a glorious flame that caused the tyrants of the earth to quail beneath its brightness; who fought the battle of civil and religious liberty, and won it, and restored to us those liberties that a despot had trampled upon. That he did not confer upon all classes that civil and religious freedom they were entitled to,—which I hold to be so much the birthright of every man, that no state or government has a right to deprive him of it,—was not through any omission or fault of his, for I believe in my soul that had he been unfettered, and allowed to carry out the measures that his own judgment dictated, he would have extended liberty to every man, regardless of the religious creed he professed; but this he was prevented from doing, by the pressure of prejudiced and interested counsellors, who circumscribed his action, and obliged him to confine his great mind to the narrow groove their own intellects moved in. Had he the power, as he had the will, he would have extended complete civil and religious liberty to all classes of his subjects, and, as a consequence, our Roman Catholic fellow-countrymen would not now be subjected to the unjust disabilities they labour under. I trust, however,—ay, and I know,—that the day is not far distant when these disabilities shall be removed; for even now I can distinguish on the distant horizon the gleams of that enlightenment which shall yet overspread our land, and rend for ever from their limbs the fetters that now enslave them. With these remarks, Gentlemen, I propose to you the memory of William of Orange,—the soldier, the statesman, the Christian, and the gentleman."

This speech produced rather a stupefying effect upon the brethren, who, accustomed all their lives to associate King William with principles so very different from those attributed to him by young Elliott, were in doubt whether the speaker was serious in his expressed desire of honouring his memory. Besides, as the sentiments the young man had expressed were decidedly heterodox, they were afraid of compromising themselves by accepting the toast as proposed. In this perplexity they looked to their fugleman as on the previous occasion, who, understanding their object, stood up and ate the leek to the very stump, subscribing to every word young Elliott had uttered, and declaring that he had never heard King William extolled so highly before; and indeed such was the fact, for it was then and still is the custom of the Orangemen to misrepresent him as a narrow-minded bigot, who would only allow Roman Catholics as such to exist on sufferance. The toast was now drunk with due respect by all the Orangemen, and even by Father O'Flynn, who, in the course of a short speech on the occasion, endorsed every word of eulogy uttered by young Elliott, and declared that he would rather live beneath the sway of such a monarch than under the king whom he had displaced.

As it was now growing late, the company began to think of breaking up; but it was not intended by their entertainers that they should leave so abruptly; for Mrs. William Nassau Elliott, having arranged to celebrate the festive occasion by an evening party, in conformity with the custom of those days, summoned them peremptorily to the drawing room, where quite a fairy scene awaited them. Such a course in the present day, on the part of a young bride, would not only be unusual, but be considered highly indecorous. In the days, however, we treat of, simple old-fashioned customs prevailed, and people used to intermarry without resorting to all the noise and ceremony now considered essential when every little Tom Noddy takes unto himself a wife. Nor was it then considered necessary, immediately on the nuptial knot being tied, to proceed "to the country," or on a trip to England or France, regardless of the season of the year or the state of the weather, as it is by the present generation, who seem to consider the honeymoon would be incomplete, unless inaugurated with an attack of sea sickness, or accompanied throughout with the pleasant companionship of rheumatism or catarrh, neuralgia or bronchitis. So

Mrs. Alderman Elliott and her daughter, like plain, sensible people, decided on passing their honeymoons comfortably at home by their own firesides.

As the brethren entered the ball room, their astonished gaze encountered numerous sylph-like forms in pink, white, and azure, floating like houris through space, awaiting the advent of the Orangeman to lead them into captivity. The sirens were successful in their machinations to the fullest extent; for ere many minutes had elapsed, each of them had secured a captive. And now the music sounded, and dancing proceeded with admirable ardour and determination. Polkas were unknown in those days; waltzes and quadrilles, but recently imported, were not generally known; so the dances to which our young friends applied themselves were the respectable old ones known as "country dances" and "cotillons," relieved occasionally by "the three-handed reel," or the sprightly "Irish jig." The enjoyment of the young people recalled to old Bob Coates, half fuddled though he was, the recollection of poor Deborah his daughter, who, little dreaming of the great doings that were taking place, was sitting in solitude at home. He thought how happy she would be to join in the revels, and mentioned his wishes to his friend, Alderman Elliott, who, like a good fellow as he was, not only declared that she should be present, but, hailing a coach, packed the old gentleman into it, charging him to bring the young lady to the scene of action instanter. These instructions Bob Coates promptly fulfilled, and soon returned with Miss Deborah, arrayed in complete ball-room attire. To the delight of her poor old tipsy father, the alderman not only greeted her with kindness, but presented her to his wife, who received her with the greatest cordiality. He then presented her to his daughter-in-law,—the young girl with the "unnatural long nose and false ringlets," when, without a moment's hesitation, the ladies fell upon each other's neck, just as young ladies will do at the present day, and kissed each other affectionately. This effusion of love inspired Dr. O'Flynn with a conundrum, the solution of which set all the ladies blushing and using their fans, and drew forth unqualified applause, from the gentlemen. "I want to know," said the doctor, "what Christian precept do these young ladies inculcate, in kissing each other as we have seen them, and what text of Scripture do they remind us of?" and, turning to his reverend friend, Mr. Whackimwell, he appealed to him as a sound divine to solve the question.

"Oh, 'love one another,' of course," replied the gentleman addressed; but the doctor shook his head, and declared his reverend friend at fault.

"'Mercy and truth are met together, righteousness and peace have *kissed* each other,'" essayed a pretty little maid just embarked in her teens, giving chapter and verse, as a pupil would to her teacher at a Sunday school.

"Very good, my dear,—very good indeed," said the doctor, placing his hand on her head; "but, though you've made a very excellent attempt, you are still wrong; for, when our young friends kissed each other so lovingly just now, they were 'doing to each other as they would that *men* should do unto them.'"

The heartiness with which this pleasantry was received threw the doctor into an exuberance of spirits, that brought forth innumerable other lively sallies from him which kept the company in a ferment of gaiety. But the great event of the evening was a song by William Nassau Gustavus Adolphus Elliott, which that young gentleman had himself composed expressly for the occasion. He sang it to the air of a popular Irish melody, in a rich barytone, and was accompanied on the piano by his wife, who was an excellent performer. So pleased were the company both with the words and the music, that, lengthy as the song was, they insisted on his repeating it—the words were as follows, and the name of it

THE GARLAND OF ORANGE AND GREEN.

I.

Two husbandmen once, known as Orange and Green,
Had as fair an estate as there ever was seen;
With its mountains and valleys, its streamlets and sea,
'Twas a home for the happy, a land for the free.
But tho' Nature had blessed it, and on it had smiled,
The land lay neglected, all wasted and wild;
For they valued it not, but devoted their life
To anger and hatred, contention and strife.

II.

One soft summer's eve in the midst of July,
When the sun was descending, and gilding the sky
With floods of bright splendour, that shone to this world
Like banners of glory by seraphs unfurled,—
When the portals of heaven seemed ope'd for the while,
And angels of hope on poor mortals to smile,—
On that bright summer's eve these two men might be seen
Contending like demons for Orange and Green.

III.

Said Will Orange, "I hate and despise all your race,"
While he brandished his lilies in front of Green's face;
"You pitiful upstart!" then outspoke the Green,
"You are only a bodagh,* a skyte,† a shoneen.‡
Both you and your lilies beneath me I trample;
I defy and detest you, and there is a sample"—
As he said, he drew back, and dealt William a pound
That felled the fierce Orangeman down to the ground.

IV.

Will arose in a trice, and gave Green such a blow,
'Twas as Hector of Troy would deal death to the foe;
This so maddened the Green, that at Orange he flew,
And he fought with the fury of Brien Boru;
Nor was Orange less active in joining the fray,
For like a wild panther he rushed on his prey;
With his eyes flashing fire, while his blows swiftly flew,
"I can conquer," he screamed out, "a dozen like you!"

V.

As the battle grew fierce, and the fight became furious,
Their neighbour, Tom White, growing prying and curious
(And anxious to know what on earth it could mean
That was causing the noise between Orange and Green),
Clambered up a tall tree ornamenting his ground
(And commanding the country for miles all around),
And he there saw the two, in that bright summer weather,
Like beasts of the forest contending together!

---

* An Irish word, signifying a *parvenu*, an upstart.

† A contemptuous term, prevalent amongst all classes in the North of Ireland, for a conceited, empty-headed man.

‡ An Irish word, meaning a shabby, mean fellow.

VI.

"Are you mad?" exclaimed White; "why, what is it you mean?
This is scandalous conduct, friends Orange and Green!
'Stead of toiling, and tilling, and minding your farm,
You fill the whole neighbourhood round with alarm.
Come into my garden, and tell me, I pray,
Why is it so fiercely you fight on this day?"
Here by tacit consent they suspended their fight,
And obeyed the request of their friend Thomas White.

VII.

As they met at the gate, White took each by the hand,
And with kindness and love led them over his land;
While they told him, with shame, that the fight he had seen
All arose from disputes about Orange and Green.
"Come, and roam," said their friend, "thro' this garden of mine,
And see how the two brilliant colours combine;
With what labour and care I my garden have tended;
And how sweetly the Green and the Orange I've blended."

VIII.

Oh! a garden of bliss was this place of Tom White—
A bower of roses—a land of delight;
Here Nature was robed in her grandeur and sheen,
In purple and orange, blue, crimson, and green;
Here the bright golden Lily raised proudly its head;
Next the brilliant Verbena with purple and red,
Pelargoniums, Anemones, Calceolarias,
Gillies, Carnations, and gay Cinerarias;

IX.

Here the richest and rarest of fruits could be found
In a wealth of profusion all clustering around—
The nectarine sweet, and the apricot rare,
The ripe ruddy apple, the smooth yellow pear,

The soft blooming peaches, and bright blushing cherries,
With clusters of all kinds of ripe rosy berries;
And the plum tree luxuriantly flourished around,
With its burden of fruit bowing down to the ground.

X.

And like children rejoicing they roamed thro' the bowers,
Gladdened here with its fruits, overjoyed with its flowers;
Fresh beauties appeared in each grotto, each glade,
The vistas, cool fountains, the lights and the shade;
And, as buoyant and happy they wandered along,
They surprised in a conclave the sweet birds of song,
Who in raptures of joy were combining to raise
Loud anthems to Heaven of gladness and praise.

XI.

As the concert broke up, all the choristers spread,
Waking up the whole garden with joy as they fled;
And the blackbird and thrush, as they winged their swift flight,
They carolled aloud their wild song of delight;
And the linnets and finches, dispersed thro' the grove,
Warbled out to their mates their fond burden of love;
While two doves in the distance joined in with a cooing,
As gentle and soft as two young lovers wooing.

XII.

"Oh," said Will to his friend, with delight in his face,
"This garden of your's is a beautiful place;
In this Eden of bliss, 'mid these bowers of gladness,
I ne'er could know grief, nor be burdened with sadness."
"It reminds me," said Green (with a fanciful notion),
"Of some isle of enchantment sprung up from the ocean,
That some bountiful genius took under his care,
Your flowers are so gorgeous, your fruits are so rare."

XIII.

"Now, tell us," said Will, "by what means, or what powers,
You came to be lord of these bright blooming bowers."
Then answered Tom White, in his blunt, honest style,
"'Twas by labour and toil that I made my land smile.
When first I possessed it, 'twas sterile and bare,
But I gave it good husbandry, culture, and care;
For 'twas working, and toiling, and tilling, I've been,
While you were disputing for Orange and Green.

XIV.

"And it lies with you both to transform your land
Into all that is beautiful, graceful, and grand;
But you've need to work hard, bear privation and care,
To meet disappointments,—yet never despair.
Above all, you must love and bear much from each other,
And be unto each like as brother to brother:
You must work, my friends, hard, and be ne'er again seen
Neglecting your garden for Orange or Green.

XV.

"There's my hand, Will!" said Green, "may it wither and fail,
If you or your lilies I e'er shall assail;
You may grow, you may plant, your bright flowers as you will,
Nay, I'll help you to rear them—there's my hand, brother Bill."
"And I," said Will Orange, accepting his hand,
While with sadness he looked towards his own wasted land,
"Will so cherish the Green, and so tend it the while,
That our land shall be famed as the Emerald Isle!"

XVI.

So to work they both went, with their strength and their might,
That their garden might bloom like their friend's, Thomas White.
As they toiled, and they laboured, and worked, with a will,
"This is better than fighting!" cried out Orange Bill.

He was answered by Green, who was guiding the plough,
As he wiped off the big drops of sweat from his brow,
"Oh, I cannot but think, Will, the fools we have been
To have quarrelled so oft' about Orange and Green!"

XVII.

And they quarrelled no more, nor e'er gave way to strife,
But were true to their land all the rest of their life;
And soon they were able to gaze with delight
On their garden, that bloomed like their neighbour's, Tom White
And their children grew up to rejoice with each other
That their fathers became unto each like a brother,
When their feuds and their quarrels for ever were ended,
And the Green and the Orange together were blended!

Never did the quondam widow look lovelier than on this auspicious occasion. She had dispensed with her cap, so that her rich dark hair was seen in its full luxuriance, while a dress of elegant design displayed her tall and splendid figure to the greatest advantage; for the modern abominations of hoops were then unknown; ladies dressed themselves at the time naturally and tastefully, unlike their sisters of the present day, who seem to consider the sole object of dress is to display the fabrics that compose it, instead of their own lithe and graceful forms; so that our modern ladies, instead of appearing as ornaments to creation, as God intended them, go forth as if made up for a masquerade,—themselves nothing, their dress everything. Like itinerant advertisements, employed by drapers for exhibiting their wares, they parade themselves divested of the natural grace and dignity belonging to the sex—melancholy caricatures of their lovely selves. So general was the sensation Mrs. Alderman Elliott created, that she diverted old Bob Coates's attention from another lady with a long neck—yclept the bottle—to whom, as the reader knows, he was devotedly attached. In the course of the night, the old veteran, who had still some of "the salt of his youth" about him, took the alderman aside, and assured him that, now that he had seen Mrs. Elliott to be "the stunning fine woman" she was, he not only did not blame him, but gave him credit for his choice; for, "Whip me soundly," said the hoary old sinner, "if I wouldn't have done the same myself!"

Miss Deborah Coates, now reconciled to the defection of young Elliott, no longer saw Kate through the false medium which the green eyes of jealousy had presented her; and in the course of the evening took occasion to inform her father that she had been quite mistaken in the opinion she had at first formed of that young lady, which must have arisen, she declared, from having glanced at her in the first instance in an oblique direction, but now that she had had a right opportunity of seeing her, she found her to be not only beautiful, but amiable and accomplished withal. Poor Debby, who was quite sincere in what she now stated, was happy to find favour in the eyes of one of the brethren, who attached himself to her the whole evening, and largely assisted to console her for the supposed loss she had sustained in the unexpected marriage of William Nassau Elliott.

But the night now draws to a close, and our friends

must separate; for in those good old times evening parties were what their names imported, and the company attending them separated at what in our days would be considered ridiculously early hours, being in fact the time when modern parties begin; and so it came to pass that at a wholesome, seasonable hour, our friends separated, well pleased with themselves and each other.

CHAPTER X.

> "Come, send round the wine, and leave points of belief
> To simpleton sages and reasoning fools;
> This moment's a flower too fair and too brief
> To be withered and stained by the dust of the schools."

THE marriage of Alderman Elliott spread much alarm and commotion throughout Orangedom. From his wealth, his high character, and his hitherto unswerving allegiance, he had hitherto proved a tower of strength to the party; but now that he had intermarried with a Roman Catholic, his actual defection from its ranks was looked forward to as by no means improbable. As time wore on, the brethren found that their apprehensions were not without foundation; for Elliott continued to absent himself from the Lodge, although reminded by Bob Coates that his attendance there was looked forward to with impatience. The fact was, that having given up the degrading habit of punch drinking, which, owing to his connexion with the Orange fraternity, he had been obliged to indulge in, and having separated himself from the stupid, besotted companions he used to waste his time with, his naturally fine mind assumed its healthy tone, so that he was enabled clearly and impartially to consider the nature, scope, and tendency of the Orange confederation, the position it assumed, and the consequences resulting from it. In the course of his deliberations he reviewed his whole life, and looked back upon the history of his country for the previous thirty years—of which he had a personal knowledge—and the following were the conclusions he arrived at:—That the Orange confederacy, to which he had been so long blindly attached, was an unnecessary, corrupt, and mischievous organization,—detrimental, in the highest degree, to the spread and progress of Protestantism; that it was fraught with ruinous consequences to Ireland as a nation; and that, so far from being a strength or support, it was a positive weakness to the British Empire; that its tendency was to promote and foster sectarian animosity, and to spread distrust and disunion amongst men whose interest it was to live together in peace and unity; that in the name of religion it performed the work of Satan more effectually than the most active agents of Lucifer ever succeeded in accomplishing; that his whole life, politically speaking, had been a great mistake,—inasmuch as, while intending to promote the prosperity of his country, and the diffusion throughout it of true religion, he had been assisting to promote results the very opposite; and that, for all these reasons, he would now, even though it might be at the eleventh hour, make the best atonement he could by dissevering himself from the Orange cause.

When it was found that he was not returning to the Lodge, and the rumour spread that he was changing his opinions, the members of "the Grand Lodge of the Purple Arch and the Scarlet Banner" held a special sitting, at which, aided as usual by abundant libations of "King Billy's cordial"—for they never met without first baptizing themselves well with it—they discussed the momentous matter, and took counsel as to the most advisable means to be adopted

"To lure the tassel gentle back again,"

and regain the truant; for Elliott had been their idol; his gentlemanly manner, and kind and genial nature, lent such harmony to their meetings, that no disagreement or discord ever arose amongst them; while his purse was ever open to contribute to the support of the cause, to which his name and character imparted a respectability and importance it could never otherwise have attained. Without him it was feared their Lodge—composed at it was, for the most part, of a coterie of miserable drunken debauchees, banded together only by the love of drink, and an insane hatred of Popery and of all who differed from them in their fanatical opinions—must either cease to exist, or become a disorganized and broken clique. Before deciding as to how they should act, they arranged to communicate with the members of the Dublin Corporation who were colleagues of their friend David Elliott, and were all of the right true blue stamp; accordingly, two of the brethren were selected to confer with the Corporation on the subject. Not less shocked were the civic dignitaries at the doleful intelligence of Alderman Elliott's desertion from the Orange ranks: such a man they could not now afford to lose; for these were troublous times. A powerful though peaceful agitation had been set on foot by the Roman Catholics for the assertion and attainment of their rights, and the removal of the galling disabilities they laboured under; while at the same time strong symptoms of disaffection began to appear amongst the rank and file of the Orange party. The leaven of political truth was operating steadily and surely amongst the Protestant community, who were growing weary of the intolerant opinions that prevailed. The violent Orange party saw with alarm that the cherished fabric they had so long striven to uphold was beginning to display signs of a speedy downfal. Seeing that Catholic Emancipation was looming in the future, they endeavoured by every means that bigotry and blind intolerance could suggest to avert the dreaded evil, or at least to stave it off to as remote a day as possible. Not only were their prejudices but their self-interest involved in the struggle; for by the removal of the civil disabilities that Catholics at the time laboured under, the members of that creed would become entitled to share in the "loaves and fishes" of the State, from which they had hitherto been rigidly excluded. Under all these circumstances, it was with real alarm that the Tory party saw the intelligence and rapidly increasing wealth of the Roman Catholic community, as well as the decided change that was taking place in public opinion. With disgust and horror they looked forward to the time when the Romanist should stand on an equality with themselves,—a day, it was too plain, that was not far distant. Daniel O'Connell, then a young man in the vigour of manhood, had just then stepped forth from the ranks of the people to organize and command the legions he was afterwards to crown with victory. Like a young chieftain, conscious of his strength, yet anxious before entering into a formal engagement to learn the power and calibre of his foes, he sharpened his sword and girded up his loins for the contest, contenting himself at first with light skirmishes, which, while teaching him how to apply his skill to the best advantage, showed him also the exact class of men he had to deal with, and the right method of using his weapons against them; continuing all the time, with surpassing eloquence, and an energy that never wearied, to expose the wrongs and disabilities that he and his fellow-Catholics laboured under,—appealing thus, by peaceful and constitutional means, to the justice of the Imperial Parliament to rive the fetters from their limbs. It was thus he cultivated and matured those splendid intellectual powers which he afterwards wielded with such tremendous effect. Beneath the force of his unanswerable arguments, the minds of men were becoming enlightened, and prepared for the great change that afterwards took place; for every word of truth, when rightly uttered, is like a grain of seed cast upon the wind, certain to take root and fructify somewhere.

After a vast deal of deliberation, the members of the Corporation, in concert with those of the Orange Lodge, decided on pursuing a very artful course to win back their truant brother. It was a cunningly devised scheme, showing that they who originated it thoroughly understood human nature, or at least one phase of it. To anticipate his defection from the cause, because he had married a Roman Catholic, would have been in the highest degree impolitic; it would, in fact, be suggesting to him the very course they did not wish him to follow. No; they would not allow him to think that they doubted his fealty, or questioned for a moment his unswerving adherence to their ranks; but, on the contrary, they would give him ample proof that they had full confidence in him, and looked upon him as still their own.

The great testimonial mania, which has since expanded itself into its present vast dimensions, had just then set in, having been originated by an ambitious parish clerk, thirsting for notoriety and fame, who, backed by the beadle, triumphantly succeeded in face of a powerful though passive opposition, in levying off the parishioners, by way of voluntary contribution, a sum of money wherewith to present a certain tax collector with a silver inkstand, in token of his meritorious public services.

"If a tax gatherer," the Orangemen argued, "who was known amongst the Hebrews by the opprobrious epithet of 'a publican and a sinner,' and who in no country has ever been a popular character, was deemed worthy of a testimonial, why should not Alderman Elliott the Orangeman—the genial good fellow and firm loyalist—have his testimonial also, and on such an auspicious occasion, too, as his marriage." He should have one, for which they would all subscribe liberally. They would present him with a splendid service of plate, upon which should be emblazoned his services to the Orange party, and their admiration of his character and public conduct. By this course they would gratify his vanity, and secure his gratitude; the result must be, that he could not think of severing himself from men who thought so highly of his character. A subscription was accordingly opened, and in a short time a large sum was collected, with which they procured a handsome service of plate, upon which were chased the Elliott Arms, tastefully festooned with Orange lilies. A deputation, consisting of the following gentlemen, was selected to wait upon our hero, and present him with the gift:—The first and greatest man amongst them was Sir Toby Jenkins, a prosperous merchant tailor, and a brother alderman of Elliott's,—a gentleman, we are bound to admit, both by character and conduct, and, but for his rabid Orangeism, an amiable and excellent man. Next to him was Mr. Sheriff Flooker, a soap-boiler and chandler,—a man much esteemed by all classes, being a well-meaning, good sort of fellow; but having, in addition to his Orangeism, the failing, which often rendered him ridiculous, of making light of the calling to which he owed his position in society,—deploring it as a misfortune that, owing to the vulgarity of a distant relation, he had been brought up to the trade he followed. He was fond of tracing his ancestry back through his mother to Athelstan, the Anglo-Saxon king, whose blood, he used exultingly to declare, tingled through his veins; yet there were people living who knew him to be ignorant of the pedigree of either his father or mother, or even of their names, inasmuch as he had been nurtured in the Foundling Hospital, which flourished in James's-street, not far from where Alderman Elliott resided. Our next is an apothecary named Dempsey, generally known as Doctor Dempsey, an ex-sheriff, and a member of the Guild of Barber Surgeons; for the old corporation of Dublin consisted of representatives from the various trades or guilds, who were supposed to constitute the city. Dempsey was a hospitable, good-natured fellow, but rather given to cant. He did a more extensive business than any other of the profession in Dublin. Most of the old ladies of the city had their medicines compounded at his establishment; for, while assured of their curative properties, they felt that they swallowed the good man's blessing with every dose they took. It used to be a standing joke amongst Dr. Dempsey's friends, that, however largely his physic was patronized by others, he was never known to swallow any of it himself. We have next a Mr. Cornelius Crawley, or Con Crawley, as he was more generally called,—a noisy but illiterate common-councilman, who, in right of his wealth, and of his bigotry and fanaticism—for it would be a desecration to use the term Protestantism in connexion with him—held a prominent position in the Corporation. A son of Crispin, he omitted no opportunity of reminding his hearers that he belonged to the Guild of Shoemakers, and that his father before him was connected with the same distinguished body. Having taken an active part in getting up the testimonial to our hero, and being naturally an officious, obtrusive man, the committee having the management of the undertaking were obliged to place him upon the deputation. Crawley was a shallow, miserable bigot of the lowest type, and one of the most irascible men that ever breathed. The last member consisted of our old friend Bob Coates, who, owing to his relationship to Alderman Elliott, and his unshaken loyalty, must necessarily be included.

The deputation so constituted was accompanied by a reporter belonging to a local newspaper, who attended as well in his official capacity as in that of a personal friend and brother Orangeman of our hero. This person, whose name was Robinson, and who was well known at the time as "Jack Robinson," was a humorous little personage, standing scarcely five feet high in his boots, who delighted in mischief, and was the merriest fellow that ever lived. To the most consummate assurance and unblushing impudence he added an imperturbable good humour, rendering him proof against rebuke or insult. And indeed this quality was most necessary to him; for Jack Robinson was an inveterate punster, and was never known to lose an opportunity, no matter at whose expense, of indulging in his jokes and witticisms.

The presentation, which was quite a grand and solemn affair, took place by appointment in a drawing room in Alderman Elliott's house, and was accompanied by an address printed on white satin. As this document is not now to be found amongst the archives of the present

Corporation of Dublin, and as it is a curiosity in its way, we give it *in extenso* :—

"BELOVED SIR AND BROTHER,

"We, your fellow-Orangemen and labourers in the sacred cause of upholding Protestant ascendancy in Church and State, and discountenancing Popery and its concomitant evils, congratulate you on the auspicious occasion of your marriage with the amiable and accomplished lady who is now your wife, and whom we may in future regard as the sleeping partner of your eminent mercantile establishment. Sincerely do we trust that the union may prove a lasting source of happiness to you both, and enable yourself, in conjunction with us, the more manfully to contend for 'the constitution, the whole constitution, and nothing but the constitution,'—and to assist us in trampling out from the body politic the cancer of Popery,

"'The thought whereof
'Doth like a poisonous mineral gnaw our inwards.'

"In presenting you with our congratulations, we beg of you to accept as a more substantial though humble token of our regard, and of our admiration of your long and consistent advocacy of the sacred cause, the accompanying service of plate, which, while recalling to your memory your old friends and brother-Orangemen, will never fail, we trust, to remind you of 'the glorious, pious, and immortal memory of the great and good King William, who saved us from Popery, slavery, knavery, brass money, wooden shoes, black bread and onions, and corns and bunions.'

"Heartily wishing you and your bride health, long life, and happiness, and praying also for a speedy downfal to Pope and Popery, we say, God bless you!

"Signed on behalf of the Loyal Corporation of Dublin, and the Orangemen of Ireland, by

"TOBIAS JENKINS, *Knight*, Alderman, Guild of Tailors; and Brother of the Schomberg Lodge.

"MOSES FLOOKER, *Sheriff*, Guild of Chandlers; Brother of the 'No Surrender Lodge.'

"EBENEZER DEMPSEY, Common-councilman, Guild of Barber Surgeons, and Brother of the 'No Popery Lodge.'

"CORNELIUS CRAWLEY, Common-councilman, Guild of Shoemakers; Brother and Deputy Chairman of the 'Grand Lodge of the Purple Arch and the Scarlet Banner.'

"ROBERT COATES, Warden of the Grand Lodge of P. A. and S. B.

"JOHN ROBINSON, Brother of the 'Free and Easy Lodge,' and Honorary Member of the 'Croppy lie down Lodge,' the Grand Lodge of P. A. and S. B. &c."

It had been arranged that this address should be read to Alderman Elliott by his brother alderman, Sir Toby

Jenkins; but Mr. Crawley, with the assumption that ever accompanies ignorance, having insisted on doing so, the worthy knight gave precedence to him. Having, after numerous blunders and a contempt for pronunciation truly entertaining, read the document through, he handed it to our hero, looking round as he did so for that applause which the able manner he had acquitted himself entitled him to; but which, however, to his mortification was not accorded him.

Our hero now felt much embarrassed as to the course he should adopt. He could not concur in the address just read to him, every line of which met with his condemnation; nor could he accept the testimonial on the terms it was presented to him. Feeling, however, that both address and testimonial were the spontaneous offerings of friendship and regard, he was reluctant to refuse either. As it was necessary, however, that he should make some reply to the address, for which his friends were now anxiously waiting, he replied to them as follows:—"Gentlemen, I thank you all heartily for the handsome and very valuable present you have offered me, which I assure you I am totally unaware of having merited."

"No, no, no!" proceeded from several of his hearers.

"Much, however," continued Elliott, "as I value the gift; and grateful as I feel to you for having presented it, I cannot think of accepting it without making some observations; after which, should you still think me worthy of it, I shall retain the present with pleasure, and shall carefully treasure it, for the sake of all the kind friends who have bestowed it, whose esteem and friendship I trust I shall never cease to possess."

"Hear, hear! bravo!" exclaimed his friends.

"Gentlemen," continued the alderman, "I would not act candidly towards you, nor do justice to myself, if I did not assure you that I consider the address you have just read to me most objectionable, if not offensive, and, to say the least of it, indicative of very bad taste."

"How's that—how's that?" asked Crawley: "to my mind it's the complatest bit o' writin I ever had the privilege of perusing."

Here Sir Toby Jenkins and others interposed, declaring that they had taken no part in the preparation of the address in question, which in fact was the joint production of Flooker, Dempsey, and Crawley.

"From the tone of this address," continued Elliott, "you appear altogether to ignore the fact, which I am sure you must be aware of, that the lady who is now my wife is a Roman Catholic."

"Ay, ay,—there ye put your foot in it," cried Crawley; "for ye well know, Alderman, 'tis the rule amongst us not to marry a Papist."

Unheeding the remarks of Crawley, whom Elliott held in supreme contempt, he was about to proceed; when several of his friends assured him that they were well aware of the fact he had alluded to, but that nothing was farther from their thoughts than to insult him, or wound his feelings.

"I am sure of that," returned Elliott, quickly; "for

I cannot and will not believe that the men with whom I have been associated all my life, and towards whom I have always borne the sincerest friendship, would wilfully offend either me or mine."

"Hear, hear! bravo!" again escaped from most of his hearers.

"Gentlemen," continued our friend, "if from the remarks I am about to make, you consider I am less sincerely a Protestant than I have hitherto been, you will labour under a great mistake indeed. I am still a true and conscientious Protestant, and shall ever I believe remain one; but, while holding these convictions, I shall never attempt to deride or contemn the religious convictions of my Roman Catholic neighbours, who are as sincerely attached to their form of worship as we are to ours."

"I can't make out what you're driving at, Alderman, at all!" exclaimed Crawley, growing impatient.

"Gentlemen, although my wife, as you know, is a Roman Catholic, let me also assure you that she is a Christian, and a good one," said Elliott. "Let me add, too, that I cannot see what necessity there was for introducing the religious element at all into your address; nor can I see why the religion professed by four-fifths of the people of Ireland should be termed a 'cancer to the body politic,' as you have characterized it. Under all the circumstances it would, I think, have been better, and certainly more considerate towards me, to have made no reference at all to the subject."

"Why is that, Brother Elliott?" asked some of the

brethren; while Crawley muttered, "The cloven foot is appearing."

"But, Gentlemen, leaving religion for the present aside, there is another subject which I must now refer to," continued Elliott; "the Testimonial you bestow upon me, as appears from your address, emanates from you clearly under the belief that I am still an Orangeman."

"Hear! hear! hear!" escaped from several voices.

"My friends, I must undeceive you there," said Elliott; "for I have determined to withdraw from the Orange Association, and I am no longer an Orangeman."

"There—the murdher's out!" screamed Crawley: "I knew all along it would come to this. There's what follows when a man allows himself to be seduced and bamboozled by the wiles and palaver of a smooth-fatured famale."

"This is grievous news, Brother Elliott," replied Sir Toby Jenkins. "Will you inform us what are the reasons that have induced you to renounce opinions you have hitherto so consistently entertained?"

"Ay, ay—we'd like to hear them," said Sheriff Flooker.

"It is due both to you and myself that I should inform you of them," returned Alderman Elliott. "Gentlemen, I have decided on ceasing to be an Orangeman, because, as a sincere Protestant, I do not wish to see the faith which our fathers contended for and followed in piety and truth dragged through the mire, and made the stalking-horse of faction,—a medium for evoking the worst passions that can degrade our nature; because I would not have religion, the mention of which should still our hearts, subdue our passions, and lead us to think with awe and reverence of the great Being who holds us in the hollow of his hand, made the watchword of party,—a pivot for political hacks and unscrupulous partisans to work upon, and carry out their wretched machinations."

"I never heerd the likes o' this in all me life," interrupted Con Crawley, appealing to his brother Orangemen with the air of a man who had sustained the deepest though unmerited injury. "To hear the loyal Orangemen of Ireland thus alluded to, and to hear the sacred cause to which ever sence I joined the Guild of Shoemakers I've been devoted to made worse nor nothing of, is more nor flesh or blood can bear. May God forgive ye, David Elliott, but I never will."

"These are hard words, Elliott," interposed Flooker; "I cannot for the life of me see how you are warranted in asserting them."

"Your language, Alderman, is to me incomprehensible," exclaimed Dr. Dempsey. "How can you connect the dreadful results you speak of with Orangeism? Look at our rules, with which no one is better acquainted than yourself; do they not inculcate brotherly love towards ourselves, and good will toward all men? Why, they are a whole treasury of Christian knowledge."

"My dear fellow," rejoined Elliott, "let us be candid at least amongst ourselves, and have no hypocrisy. I think you will admit that I know what Orangeism is, and what its professors are."

"Hear, hear!" was the response.

"Well, then, I say to you this, that it is as gross an imposition as was ever indulged in, to mislead the public, or ourselves, by representing Orangeism as a society in any way tending to the promotion of religion. I care not what your rules are, though they breathed all the piety and Christianity that saints or angels ever uttered, the effects of the organization—I may say the natural effects of it—are not only to discountenance religion, but to promote and spread irreligion, and all its train of evils,—intemperance, indolence, and immorality; that its tendency is to engender and foster 'envy, hatred and malice, and all uncharitableness,' towards our Roman Catholic neighbours, and 'pride, vainglory, and hypocrisy' in ourselves. Is not this all true? Look at us as we stand in this room—must we not all more or less plead guilty to this charge? Is there one amongst us who can even call himself a moral man,—not to say a religious one,—or who can honestly say that he has tried to become so? Have we not all, while connected with our Orange Lodges, neglected our religion, deserted our homes, and led bad and irregular lives?"

"Oh, Alderman, I don't understand your remarks," broke in Doctor Dempsey, placing his hand across his bosom, and throwing up the whites of his eyes; "I thank my God, I have always walked in the right way."

"Let us take an example now," said Elliott, carried

away by his subject. "Look at the North of Ireland: there you will find a people industrious, honest, intelligent, and thrifty. I speak generally, for I include both Protestant and Catholic. Go amongst these people, and you will find them, with the exceptions I shall refer to, an example to the entire country,—moral, religious, and law-observing. They would live all their lives together in brotherly love, for there is a sort of clanship amongst them that makes them cling to each other irrespective of creed or party, were it not that there is an element of strife amongst them, smouldering in their bosoms, that periodically turns these people, who would otherwise live in amity and peace together, into very demons! What is that element? It is Orangeism, and nothing else."

A perfect howl of rage here escaped from Crawley, who indulged in the most violent language, declaring that Elliott himself was a demon for having made such an assertion. His companions also dissented from Elliott's remarks, but in a less violent manner.

"And what is Orangeism?" continued Elliott, impetuously. "Let us look at it. More than one hundred and twenty years ago, a bigot, a tyrant, and a despot—whom neither advice, experience, nor adversity could teach—persisted in depriving us of our liberties; when I say 'us,' I mean both Catholic and Protestant; for, though he was a Papist, he would have crushed the liberties of the Roman Catholic the same as the Protestant, if he could. The British nation, with that glorious love of liberty which has ever distinguished it, rose as one man against the oppressor, and summoned to their aid the valiant Prince of Orange, who with a small but gallant band had upheld liberty upon the Continent. But how were matters circumstanced in Ireland? Four-fifths of the population were Roman Catholics, who had been treated like helots; their creed—and that, too, a Christian one—ignored, and almost proscribed; all avenues to honour and advancement closed against them; while the religion professed by the remaining fifth of the people was the recognised one of the State, its professors alone being eligible for place, power, or position. A more anomalous state of things the history of civilization has never afforded. Well, King James—rejected by the English—naturally looks for sympathy to his Irish people, whose religion he promised to maintain and uphold, and whose civil disabilities to remove. Was it not natural, then, that the oppressed and down-trodden Irish Romanists should rally round the banner of the man who promised to be their deliverer? And this they did, not for love of the man, but because in very desperation they hoped through his agency to obtain that liberty the dominant party denied them. Would not Protestants, under like circumstances, have done exactly the same? Well, then, James was defeated; and here let me observe, that it is no reproach to our countrymen, who have proved their prowess on a hundred battle-fields, that, commanded by a poltroon, they were unable to withstand the flower of English chivalry, led as it was by such a hero as William of Orange. The kingly prerogative was now finally settled, and constitutional government established. All this happened one hundred and twenty years ago; yet how do matters stand? Not satisfied with their victory, the Orangemen of Ulster persist, year after year, in reminding their Roman Catholic countrymen of their triumph. To-day they are at peace with their neighbour, who desires only to live in amity with them; yet to-morrow they turn out—because it is the anniversary of that contest which should ages ago have been buried in oblivion—and brandish their symbols of triumph in his face, and sound in his ears the tocsin of defiance. They say in effect to him, 'Though it is now more than a century ago since our fathers and yours fought together, and although five generations have passed away since then, and the occasion that gave rise to the struggle has passed away too, we will not let the matter rest—we will still continue to glory in the victory as though it only took place yesterday, and will taunt you still for your defeat; and we will show you that we are ready now to revive the quarrel, and renew the fight.' This is what the Orangemen annually do in the North of Ireland, and what you in a quieter way do here in Dublin also. What are the consequences of these wretched broils? As a matter of course, Roman Catholics accept the challenge—if they did not do so, they would not be made of flesh and blood like ourselves; and then we see men, ay, and women, too—for the violence of party feeling unsexes them for the time—who but yesterday lived peacefully together, following industriously their callings, give way to every evil passion that degrades humanity, and meet together in deadly strife, ending in bloodshed, in massacre, and in—death!

> "'O, the offence is rank, it smells to heaven;
> It hath the primal eldest curse upon 't,
> A brother's murder!'

These are the fruits of Orangeism in the North; and we should have the same here, were it not that you are so outnumbered by Roman Catholics that you dare not defy them as your Northern brother-Orangemen do. These, I say, are the fruits of Orangeism; and we have it on the highest authority, that it is by men's fruits they should be judged."

And now Elliott, almost breathless with excitement, ceased for the present to speak. During the delivery of the speech he was frequently interrupted by Con Crawley, who at every pause joined in with some remark, like the chorus in a Greek play, but with this difference—that in the one case the object is to illustrate and embellish, but in Crawley's the intention was to derange and distract.

"I tell you what it is, Elliott!" he exclaimed, when our hero had concluded, "you may abuse and blackguard us Orangemen as you like, but, for all that, we are the only rale loyal men in Ireland. We're the proudest feather in England's cap; for we're able to hold the country against every disloyal Papist in it, were they fifty to one. England couldn't do without us, and well she knows that."

"Pooh!" returned Elliott; "if the British Government acted wisely they'd reduce you to insignificance. Your loyalty is not worth the price you exact for it."

"What price?—what do you mean, Elliott?" asked several of his hearers.

"I mean that your loyalty, as you call it, is purchased by the disloyalty, passive though it be, of every Roman Catholic in the country."

"Be gonnies!" exclaimed Crawley, "I really don't know whether I stand on my head or my feet. I never heerd the likes o' this in all my life."

"You are loyal," continued Elliott, "so long as your Roman Catholic fellow-countrymen are kept enslaved and degraded. And what is that loyalty, you boast so much of, worth? Your numbers do not exceed two hundred thousand; for Orangeism does not represent the entire Protestant population of Ireland,—God forbid that it should! It is only an excrescence, that defaces our Protestantism. Well, then, take your numbers at two hundred thousand, and my answer is—that I would rather have the loyalty of five millions of people (for that is about the number of Catholics in the country) than the conditional loyalty of a handful of such fanatics as you. For the devoted loyalty of these five millions England could secure to-morrow, if she would only place the Catholic politically on an equality with you."

"You'd strengthen England with Papists, would you?" broke in Sheriff Flooker; "that would be trusting to a broken reed. I tell you, Elliott, that a Papist's loyalty is worthless, for it cannot be depended on. No Papist ever was, or could be, loyal to a Protestant government; his soul is not his own, but his priest's, who hates and curses England as Satan does the blessed sun. No Papist, I repeat, ever was, or ever will be, true to a Protestant sovereign."

A murmur of applause followed this speech, to which Elliott replied—

"Flooker, I am surprised that a man of your good sense could be so blinded by prejudice, and so forgetful of facts that have taken place within your own recollection, as to make the assertion you have just uttered. You say that no Catholic ever was, or could be, true to a Protestant government?"

"Hear! hear!" exclaimed Flooker.

"Tell me, Flooker," continued Elliott, "were the Irish soldiers who assisted Wellington to drive the French from the Peninsula, and who formed at least a third of his forces, loyal to the British government? Did you ever hear that they showed less devotion to their flag than their Scotch and English comrades? Did our own Eighty-eighth, when it tore down from the bloodstained walls of Badajos the Imperial eagles, and placed the British ensign there, show themselves traitors to the English Crown? Did our gallant countrymen show disloyalty to Protestant England when they helped at Vittoria to break the proud chivalry of France, and ultimately drive its veteran legions across the Pyrenees a scattered host? Has not the Irish soldier—that disloyal Papist, as you call him—borne his part faithfully and bravely in restoring peace to Europe, and placing England where she now stands—upon the pinnacle of greatness? And should Napoleon Buonaparte—who like a caged lion lies immured within his little isle of Elba, where his mighty spirit now chafes and frets itself—ever return to France, and spread again the flame of war, where will England look for true and dauntless hearts to aid her in crushing once more the mighty chieftain? Will she not again appeal to these Irish Papists you so contemptuously allude to? Away, then, with your imputation of disloyalty, which is as ungrateful as it is unjust, and a foul and groundless libel upon our Catholic fellow-countrymen!"

A scene of indescribable uproar followed this speech; for Elliott's hearers, finding themselves worsted in the argument, began, as people are apt to do under such circumstances, to lose their tempers. Every one endeavoured to gain a hearing,—the noisiest amongst them being Crawley, who, in his frantic efforts to be heard, roared like an angry bull, and gesticulated like a madman. At length the parties, exhausted by their own violence, were reduced to silence, when Elliott arose, and continued—

"Gentlemen, I believe we have made a grave mistake in treating Romanism, as we have hitherto done, as no religion at all, or worse than no religion. I think we should have acted towards the Catholics as though they were our fellow-Christians, and as members of the Christian Church, entitled to the same privileges as ourselves."

"I say—no!" roared Crawley; "Turk, Jew, or Atheist for me, but a Papist."

Much excitement again began to manifest itself, when Elliott interposed, and after some difficulty obtained permission to proceed.

"Gentlemen," he continued, "this is neither the time nor place, nor am I indeed the person, to pursue this subject further. I must, however, repeat that I think we are acting unjustly, not only towards our Catholic neighbours, but to ourselves, by treating them otherwise than as I have stated. There are differences in our religious views and theirs; but there are strong points of agreement also, which should cement the bonds of Christian fellowship between us."

At this attempt of Elliott to place the Romish and Protestant forms of Christianity on an equality, most of his hearers loudly expressed their dissent, while a perfect howl of rage escaped from Crawley, who characterized Romanism as "a filthy, abominable, soul-destroying heresy."

"Don't give yourself any more anxiety on that point, Con," broke in Jack Robinson; "for should *your* soul be lost, 'twill not be owing to Popery."

This was a hard hit, which Crawley keenly felt; for, besides being a drunkard, like his brother Orangeman Bob Coates, he was what is generally known as "a loose, bad-living man."

"Hold your tongue, you contemptible little sparrow!" returned Crawley, foaming with rage. "I tell you what it is," he continued, "I wouldn't enter heaven if I thought a Papist would receive admittance there."

"You'll never get the offer, Con," rejoined Jack Robinson.

"Am I to be interrupted thus by a stunted hop-o'-my-thumb like that?" roared Crawley, pointing contemptuously to Robinson, who, rubbing his hands together in a transport of delight, cried,

"Bravo! Con, bravo! I knew I'd get you up at last, —ho! ho! ho!"

"And now, my friends," continued Elliott, "let me advise you to withdraw from the Orange Society, which is an organization as vicious as it is useless."

Here the alderman was interrupted by Crawley, who exclaimed, in a whining tone—

"Oh! that I should ever live to hear the holy and blessed cause spoken of thus,—a cause which has been supported by dukes, and baronets, and knights of the garter!"

"I am well aware," replied Elliott, "that you have amongst you gentlemen of position and character, ay, and noblemen, too,—men of honour, justice, and benevolence—who have no real bigotry in their natures—who live in amity with their Roman Catholic neighbours, and would be as incapable of wilfully inflicting injury upon them as they would to themselves. The fact, however, that you have such men amongst you is the more to be deplored, for it is owing to their countenance and support that the system is maintained. If they would withdraw themselves from it, the Orange confederation would soon die a natural death, and the country would no longer be disgraced by its excesses.

As for myself, when I think of the manner in which I have wasted the past thirty years of my life through my connexion with it—when I think of the besotted life I have led; that, while continually joining in abuse of the Catholic religion, I have almost totally neglected my own—I feel thoroughly ashamed of myself. Believe me, my friends, the Orange Lodge is not the place to acquire morality or religion. Thank heaven, we have abundance of houses of worship, and plenty of able and faithful ministers to expound the Gospel there: such are the places where religion is to be learned, and they are the men to teach it. Let us, then, abandon this corrupt and mischievous confederacy; and when we meet together as Protestants, let it be in the house of God, where, while we shall be strengthened and instructed in our faith, we shall learn Christian charity and forbearance towards all men,—enabling us to look upon our Catholic neighbours, not as the monsters of bigotry, intolerance, and superstition, it has been habitual with us to regard them, but as our fellow-countrymen and Christians."

The rapidity and excitement with which Elliott uttered this speech obliged him to pause for a moment, when Dr. Dempsey replied to him—

"Why, Alderman, you entirely mistake in alleging that we hate Roman Catholics. We don't hate them; we have never hated them. Look at me—do I hate my Roman Catholic countrymen? No, I love them; I deplore their spiritual destitution; I pity their benighted condition; I weep for the condition of their immortal souls. I would lead them from the house of bondage, even as the shepherd guideth his sheep, to the land of Canaan, flowing, not with milk and honey, but with everlasting truth; I would guide them"—

"My dear fellow," interrupted Elliott, "I say again, let us have no humbug or hypocrisy. Don't you well know that Roman Catholics don't want you to lead them anywhere, and have no faith in your guidance? All they want is to be allowed the free exercise of their religion."

"Maybe it's Emancipation you'd give them?" asked Crawley, with a sneer.

"Of course it is," rejoined Elliott; "they are entitled to it, and it is a reproach to Protestants to withhold it from them."

Here Crawley, who had been for some time boiling with rage, declared that rather than see emancipation extended to the Catholics, he would see Ireland a wilderness; and that if ever England granted it, he would become her deadliest of foes. "As for you," said he to Elliott, in conclusion, "I denounce you as a traitor and a renegade! You have betrayed your party, and bartered away your faith!—and for what have you done so? For the sake of a woman! Faugh!—I despise ye, man!"

This was the signal for another scene of uproar, every one now condemning Crawley for his violent language, and he in his turn discharging the foulest abuse at his assailants. At length Jack Robinson, mounting a chair, succeeded in obtaining a hearing—

"Gentlemen!" he cried, "it is hardly fair, after strewing so thickly the flowers of eloquence around, that we should now turn our friend's house into a *bear* garden. Besides, Gentlemen, we should remember that, as Orangemen, it is our duty to deal in *civil* oranges as much as possible."

"Bravo, Jack!—Hear Jack Robinson!" cried several of his hearers.

"Gentlemen," continued Jack, "I humbly move that I do take the chair."

"And I second the motion," exclaimed Sir Toby Jenkins, anxious for any change that might put an end to the disorderly scene that was being enacted.

Jack Robinson, having now formally installed himself as chairman, called for silence, which having been accorded, he demanded of Crawley to retract the offensive language he had applied to Alderman Elliott, a demand which the other members of the deputation eagerly joined in; Sir Toby Jenkins declaring that, if that person did not comply with the request, and apologize also to their friend, he would bring the matter before the Corporation, and move his expulsion from that body. Brought to reason by the pressure thus forced upon him, Crawley began to whine and whimper, declaring that there was a combination amongst them to put him down. "I never before was charged with unparliamentary language," said he; "my father, who belonged to the Guild of Shoemakers as I do, always spoke like a Parliament man; and ever since I joined the guild I have done my endayvors to follow as I may say in his *shoes*. If my language was not parliamentary, I intended it to have been so."

"But it was not parliamentary, as you call it," said Flooker; "it was most violent and scandalous, and we insist on your withdrawing it."

"Well, since ye all insist, of coorse I must yield; I therefore withdraw any unproper words I may have used, but I reserve to myself, however, the right of *thinking* them; for though I may not call a man a spalpeen, I have yet to learn that I am not free to think him one if I choose. So far, then, as regards the alderman, I unsay what I've said, but I'll think what I think."

"Bravo, Con! that will do beautifully," returned Jack Robinson. "You may indulge in any flight of fancy you like,—even to that of thinking yourself a gentleman."

Looking daggers at Jack Robinson, Con Crawley continued,—"When a man like me, who has been five-and-twenty years a member of the Guild of Shoemakers, and whose father before him belonged to the same loyal body—when a man like me, I say, who fought for freedom in '98"——

"I say, Con," interrupted Robinson, "wasn't the corps you served in called 'the Devil's own?'"

"No, Sir, it wasn't," retorted Crawley, sharply,—"that was the Lawyers' corps, and well deserving it was of the name. I served, Sir, in Stamer's corps, and I bled in the service."

"Ay, you were wounded in the back, as you were running away from the field, and served you right."

"No, Sir, 'twas in the head I was struck, and there's

the remains of it;" and, removing the brown scratch wig that adorned his head, Con Crawley displayed his bald cranium, upon which was the cicatrice of what must once have been a serious wound.

"Pooh!" returned Robinson, "I know the mark well—'twas a blow of a pewter quart you received in a row you got into in Killeen's Tavern, for refusing to pay the reckoning."

Crawley now broke into a violent passion, and would have inflicted personal chastisement on the offender, had not Jenkins and Flooker succeeded in cooling him down.

"You little wretch!" said he, glaring across the table at his tormentor, "if you address another observation to me, I'll trounce you to within an inch of your life—I will, you wasp, I will!" and, to add force to his words, he smote the table violently with his clenched fist.

"That will do, Con!" cried Robinson. "We all know you're a *striking* character, so it's quite unnecessary to give us proof of the fact." This retort of Robinson produced a burst of laughter that restored something like good humour amongst them; when Robinson, taking advantage of the opportunity, proceeded: "Gentlemen, we have made a sad mistake in introducing politics into our proceedings; for are we not assembled solely to compliment our old friend and comrade,—a gentleman who, however he may change his politics, or modify his religious opinions, must ever remain what he has always been,—the prince of good fellows?"

"Hear, hear, hear!"—proceeded lustily from all present, save Crawley, who preserved a dogged silence.

"Gentlemen, the address which has been read to our friend was all a mistake," continued Robinson; "is it not so?"

"Yes, yes!" eagerly exclaimed Jenkins and Bob Coates.

"Such being the case, I withdraw it, and shall keep it by me as a curiosity of literature." So saying, he rolled up the satin scroll, and placed it in his pocket.

"And now," continued Robinson, "I shall, with your permission, deliver to our friend the address which ought to have been presented him."

"Bravo!—hear Jack Robinson!" exclaimed his auditors, whereupon our little friend gravely proceeded:—

"SIR AND BROTHER,

"We, your old friends and comrades, congratulate you on your marriage with the lovely and accomplished lady you have now the honour of calling your wife. In doing so, we deplore it with regret that a circumstance which brings rejoicing to your heart, should fall with sadness upon ours; for we know that, owing to your marriage, you must necessarily withdraw yourself from us. How could you desert a home, graced by such a treasure, for the poor attractions afforded by us? It grieves us to know that we shall miss you in future at the festal board, where your cheerfulness and serenity of temper have ever tended to spread harmony amongst us, and to endear you to our hearts. You are now, Sir, not an Orangeman, but a lady's man.

Engrossed as you are with a lovely white lily at home, we can well understand how faded and effete an orange lily must appear to you. May you and that charming flower long bloom and flourish together, shedding around you the perfume of purity, honour, benevolence, and truth.

"But, Sir, though you have withdrawn from us, it is far from our intention to part from you. As you will not come to our Lodge, it is our intention occasionally to visit your's; for we are well assured that you will welcome us so heartily as not only to *lodge* but *board* us also.

"With this address, we beg of you to accept, as a testimonial of our friendship, and of our appreciation of your worth, the service of plate that glitters before us, which poorly expresses the warmth of our feelings towards you. Sir, when we think of the *plates*, ay, and the excellent *dishes*, too, which you have so often presented to us—all of them well garnished with the best of good things—we cannot help feeling that the bare service of plate that we present you with is but an *empty* compliment. We leave the filling of those plates, however, to you—a task which you thoroughly understand; and, believe me, that, whenever you have done so, you shall always find us ready to assist you to *polish* them clean, so that they shall ever remain, as you now see them, bright as your own honour, and spotless as your fame.

"And now, Sir, I conclude,—wishing you and your lady health, long life, and happiness."

A burst of applause followed Jack Robinson's timely address, which had the effect of completely restoring harmony and good humour. They all now crowded round Elliott, eager to shake hands with him, and assure him of their unalterable affection. Even Crawley, carried away by the general enthusiasm, begged of our hero to make friends with him, and excuse his zeal, to which Elliott readily assented.

Alderman Elliott now arose, and, again thanking his friends for their present, insisted on their partaking of some refreshment,—feeling that, after the exciting scene that had passed, they stood in need of a glass of wine by way of a cooler.

And now Jack Robinson arose again to address them. "Gentlemen," said he, "I am about to propose a toast, which I know beforehand you will acknowledge in a bumper,—for it is that of 'Our noble selves.'"

Cheers and laughter to any amount followed this announcement.

"In doing so," continued Jack, "I cannot avoid taking notice, individually, of the illustrious persons composing this assembly. As for our worthy friend, to honour whom we have met together, it is hardly necessary that I should add anything to what I have already said. Besides, the task would be a laborious one; for on the present occasion, at all events, our friend is a *host* in himself. Let me, however, in the words of the best of *little* men, again wish joy to himself and his lady, trusting—

"'That when time, who steals their years away,
Shall steal their pleasures too,
The memory of the past shall stay,
And half their joys renew;
That, thinking ne'er of future gloom,
Those joys may always last;
For hope shall brighten days to come,
And memory gild the past.'"

"Bravo! Jack, bravo!" cried his hearers, enthusiastically.

"Our excellent friend, Sir Toby Jenkins, who ornaments the Guild of Tailors, deserves next our notice," continued Robinson; "for a worthier knight never earned his spurs. I have known him long, Gentlemen, and have ever found him the most trustful and confiding of men. Oft have I had occasion to plead to him, but never in vain, for on every occasion I succeeded in gaining my *suit*. Honour him—esteem him—patronize him. He is well worthy of support; for, though skilful at using the shears, he never will venture to *fleece* you."

"Bravo, Jack!" returned Sir Toby, laughing heartily; "but take care you don't lose your suit next time,—you're apt to let judgment go by default."

"Should I do so," returned Jack, "I'll move for a new *trial*, which I know you'll grant, and then I'll put you in for another *suit*."

"I have now to refer to Brother Dempsey, who so worthily represents the Guild of Barber Surgeons. As for his efficiency as a barber, I can say but little; for, although he is a most excellent man, he is not by any means a *keen shaver*. I undertake, however, to say, that whenever he cuts your head, he will not fail to give you a plaster. I would rather speak of our friend as a surgeon, being able to vouch for his efficiency in that capacity; for, Gentlemen, he has often *trepanned* me under his roof, where he has never failed to *cup* me freely; for, although there was no blood-letting on such occasions, he has always drawn plenty of *claret*,—a species of *black draught* our friend is rather fond of administering—though, indeed, I must say that on the times I refer to he has always 'thrown physic to the dogs.'"

Much laughter and applause followed this allusion to Doctor Dempsey, who kept open house, and was famed for his hospitality.

"And now," said Robinson, "I have to perform a task of some difficulty; for I see before me a gentleman whose eminent lineage throws mere parvenus like myself and the rest of us entirely into the shade, and whose merits, in consequence, I feel myself unable to do full justice to. I allude, as you are doubtless aware, to our respected brother, Sheriff Flooker, of the Guild of Chandlers,—a gentleman who has royal blood in his veins, being a lineal descendant of"——

"Athelstan," said Flooker, smiling with gratified pride. "We came over with Strongbow."

"Oh, King Athelstan, was it?" returned Robinson. "Gentlemen, the worthy sheriff tells us his ancestors arrived in this country with Strongbow. If I had not implicit confidence in everything that falls from him, I would have thought it must have been with *Long*-bow.

What an honour is it to have such a man amongst us? Not only is he descended from royalty, but he is royal himself; for is he not the Prince of Chandlers and the King of *Grease,*—a gentleman whose intimacy with *Windsor* is not only a source of profit to himself, but enables us all to approach our undertakings with *clean hands?*—a man of such extraordinary powers that he is able to guide and direct us in the most obscure and intricate paths; for so long as the worthy sheriff lives and flourishes, who can 'hold a *candle* to him' at lightening our darkness?"

Here Crawley, with a malicious leer at the object of Robinson's remarks, exclaimed, "That's touching you off in nate style, Flooker!" for there was an old feud between them. Crawley, whose father had been a very humble man, having carried on his handicraft in one of those monuments of antiquity which have now all but disappeared from Dublin, known as "cobblers' bulks," could not bear to hear Flooker, whose history he was aware of, boast of his lineage; and he omitted, in consequence, no opportunity of enjoying a laugh at his brother-Orangeman's expense.

"Ah, Con, my old friend, I'm coming to you," said Robinson, attracted to that person by his remarks. "Now I feel myself at home; for it's a pleasure to be able to do justice to real merit. You have all heard the brilliancy of Brother Crawley remarks, and his touching allusions to the Guild of Shoemakers. Gentlemen, if our friend has not given us on this occasion a 'feast of reason,' you all

I think will concur with me in saying that he has treated us to '*a flow of sole;*' for, though his remarks savoured strong of the *brogue*, they were highly suggestive of *polish.* May the worthy common-councilman long be spared us to improve our *understandings;* may he and his *awl* flourish, and his family *tree* take root in the soil. Until I had the privilege of hearing him to-day, I was ignorant of the fact that he was a military character—I am now, however, aware of it; for it was impossible to look upon him just now, during his occasional bursts of excitement, without being reminded of the strong likeness he bears to *Bellona*, a young lady of the most martial tendencies, but by no means remarkable for beauty: why, so warlike a character is our friend, that from the moment he divested himself of his wig, and displayed his *bullet-*head, I have thought of nothing save culverins, cannon balls, and bomb-shells. Had he not told us that during the troubles of '98 he fought under Sir William Stamer, I should have said he must have served with the *Hessians;** I am pleased, however, to find it was not so; and should ever the gentry I allude to again show their faces in this country, I trust he will be ready to help us all to *welt* them

* These mercenary troops, who gave the name to a kind of boot much worn at the period, were employed with the king's forces in suppressing the Irish rebellion; the atrocities they perpetrated on the unfortunate people during that melancholy struggle were the subject of execration over the entire country for many years after the outbreak was quelled.

soundly, so that they will very soon show us their *heels*. Of this we may all rest assured, that so long as we have Con Crawley amongst us we shall never want a *Wellington* or a *Blucher*, to enable us to put the best foot forward, and trounce any enemy that may invade our shores. Long I trust may our excellent friend be spared us; and when he has *waxed* old, and approaches his *last*, and come as it were to his *end*, may the better part of him, which I will call his *uppers*, find a resting-place with the *souls* of the weary."

Much laughter followed Robinson's allusions to Con Crawley, not so much at the matter of them, as at the manner with which that person received them; for the stupid old fellow seemed doubtful as to whether Robinson was ridiculing or complimenting him.

"And now," continued Jack Robinson, "I have only to allude to Bob Coates and myself. Bob and I are old friends and fellow-campaigners. Gentlemen, I know the powers and capabilities of our friend; and if loyalty to the British crown can be measured by the amount of 'King Billy's cordial' he is able to dispose of, I fearlessly assert that King George has not a more loyal subject in his dominions. Often have I heard my friend allude to that fluid as 'calamity water;' Gentlemen, I trust it shall never prove calamitous to him; and that, notwithstanding the extent of his libations, he shall ever enjoy health, wealth, and prosperity."

"Hear, hear, hear! bravo!" shouted his hearers, for poor Bob Coates was a general favourite.

"I have now to say a few words respecting myself,"

continued the little man; "and here I feel the greatest difficulty of all, for, gentlemen, I am a modest man—a bashful man. I am not a military character like Con Crawley, though my sympathies are all in that direction, for I shave with an *army razor*, and wear the best high-heeled *Wellington* boots; for, though my altitude precludes me from holding an elevated position in society, I wish to be looked upon as a *rising* man. In fact, I am rather a naval than a military character, seeing that I am one of the *press* gang; but, as that institution has never been popular, I shall say no more about it. I will therefore conclude by reminding you of the directions of the Prince of Denmark as to the mode of treating the players—'Let them be well used,' said the sentimental young gentleman, 'for they are the abstracts, and brief chronicles, of the time;' and so, let me remind you, gentlemen, is your friend Jack Robinson; for is he not a Reporter? 'After your death,' says the prince, 'you were better have a bad epitaph, than their ill report while you lived; use them better than they deserve, for treat every man after his desert, and who shall 'scape whipping? use them with honour and dignity; the less they deserve, the more merit is in your bounty.'"

"Bravo, Jack Robinson, bravo!" cried every one, when the little man had concluded, for he had kept them for some time in the very height of good humour and merriment. "You're a brave man, Jack," said Elliott, shaking his friend warmly by the hand, for he rightly attributed the amicable termination of the meeting to his agency.

The entire company, now quite reconciled to the departure from their body of their friend Alderman Elliott, took their departure, assuring him of their unaltered esteem. The fact really was, that Elliott's argument went home with convincing force to many of his friends, and, as will afterwards be seen, brought about the conversion of some of them.

CHAPTER XI.

"Honour, riches, marriage, blessing,
Long continuance and increasing;
Hourly joys be still upon you!
Juno sings her blessing on you;
Earth's increase and foison plenty,
Barns and garners never empty;
Vines, with clust'ring bunches growing,
Plants with goodly burden bowing:
Spring come to you, at the farthest,
In the very end of harvest!
Scarcity and want shall shun you,
Ceres' blessing so is on you."

A FEW years have elapsed since the occurrences treated of in the preceding chapters, and every day that had passed confirmed David Elliott in the wisdom of the course he had adopted both as regards his marriage, and his withdrawal from the Orange confederation. In the woman he had married he found the sweetest and most devoted wife that man has been ever blessed with. Endowed with every virtue that adorns her sex,—simple yet wise, amiable, cheerful, well-informed, and intellectual, she was at once his friend, his mentor, his guide, *his companion*. In her society he found enjoyments he had never known before, so that life seemed to afford him a foretaste of that hereafter which the Christian looks for with unfaltering faith. Instead of the votary of a sensual and grovelling superstition, whose religion consisted in the performance of senseless ceremonies, as at one period of his life he would have looked upon such a woman because a Roman Catholic, he found in her a true and practical Christian, guided in her conduct by the same motives that actuated him; and on her part she found her husband, not a degraded heretic, such as Protestants had been represented to her, but an equally sincere Christian, differing only from her in his mode of professing their common belief. And thus they journeyed on together, each esteeming the other in a moral and religious sense as the nearest to perfection that can be met with in finite humanity. Cured of the vicious habits of intemperance he once was prone to—cured also of the violent prejudices that caused him to look upon his neighbour who differed from him in religion as something monstrous in creation—blind to his virtues, but sentient to his faults—his heart is raised to God and his wondrous works; he now no longer looks upon creation through a false, distorted medium, but sees it in its real loveliness and splendour. And, oh, how blessed is the life he now leads! Nature presents to him a bright and glorious picture, wrought by the handywork of God. Every object in it has attractions for him it never had before. When he treads the fields, they seem to him to glow with brighter verdure; the flowers he once heeded not, have now unspeakable charms for him; the trees, more graceful and majestic, are clothed with richer foliage; the song of the birds is sweeter. There is music now in the purling streams; and the hum of the busy insects dancing through the air breathes to him a song of joy. The bread he eats is sweeter; sleep to him is more refreshing; and when he wakes, it is to rejoice that another day is given him, and to pour out his heart in thankfulness and praise. The fragrant breath of morning is incense wafted to him from heaven; the dew that laves the flowers is nectar from the same Omniscient source. All nature seems to rejoice, and proclaim to him the great truth that God is everywhere. When he gazes upon the heavens in their sunlight splendour, or looks upon them studded with a myriad gems by night; when he sees the boundless ocean, in its mysterious grandeur, ever moving obedient like a docile child to the Being whose immutable laws it follows; when he sees the rivers rushing onward in their course, and gazes on the lofty mountains stretching high to the heavens—an overwhelming sense of joy possesses him; for he feels that the same mighty Being who created these monuments of his enduring wisdom, also fashioned him, and sustains him with his Omnipotent hand; and while exulting in the consciousness of this, his heart swells with an overpowering sense of gratitude to Him to whom he owes so much. And how can he display that gratitude? Oh, there are a hundred ways, in this world, by which he who is sincere in such feelings can find ways to gratify them. And never did man more truly and sincerely evince his gratitude than he. "To comfort and help the weak-hearted—to raise up them that fall,—to succour, help, and comfort all that are in danger, necessity, and tribulation,"—became the darling object of his life, for which his wealth, his position, and influence afforded him unusual opportunities. And in this good work he had an able coadjutor in his wife, who entered into all his plans with her whole heart and soul. And so they pursued together their useful and beneficent career, like a rich stream that diffuses health and freshness, life and nutriment, in its course.

In all these benevolent schemes Elliott was also aided by his son; but active labour and the promotion of industrial employment was the great pursuit that occupied this young man's time. Shortly after his marriage, David Elliott, having formally taken his son into partnership, gave up the management of his establishment to him; and now the young man devoted all his energies to the extension of their trade. Under his skilful guidance, the business soon doubled; so that they were able to extend useful and profitable employment to a large number of industrious people; and this formed a source of real pleasure to them both; for they derived more satisfaction from the consciousness of affording such employment, than in the acquisition of the profits, large as they were, resulting from it. Next to these benevolent and industrial pursuits, the great object both of the father and son was to promote union, fellowship, and love amongst their countrymen—to soften down asperities, heal their quarrels, and to put an end to sectarian strife. They saw the great natural advantages that Ireland possessed in an agricultural, commercial, and geographical point of view, and the admirable materials existing for developing and utilizing them in their hardy, industrious, and intelligent fellow-countrymen; they saw that party feeling and sectarian differences were the bane of the country, and their object was to endeavour to effect such a fusion amongst Irishmen as would enable them all to pull together for the common good. But here there was a great difficulty to contend against: no such union could possibly be effected until the just claims of the Catholics were conceded. So long as five millions of their countrymen, as intelligent and as moral a people, according to their respective positions, as any country could produce, were deprived of their rights of citizenship,—so long as their revered religion was ignored and degraded, while the religion of the minority was that alone recognized by the State,—how could a nation so constituted and governed act in unison and make progress? The thing was morally impossible. As has been observed in the preceding chapter, a movement was on foot for effectuating the emancipation of the Roman Catholics. Into this both father and son threw their whole hearts and souls. Sincere Protestants as they were, they felt that, having perfect freedom of worship themselves, a stigma attached to them if they did not raise their voice in an indignant protest against the wrong that in the name of Protestantism, and under a Protestant constitution, was being perpetrated on their fellow-countrymen.

And both Elliott and his son lived to see that movement successful, and that stigma removed; for truth and justice are eternal, and will yet prevail, though tyrants and all their cunning combat against it; and with pleasure, and not with jealousy, they saw a new life infused into the Roman Catholic community, who now assumed the position in society that iniquitous laws had for centuries deprived them of; they saw the Roman Catholics rise to opulence, position, and dignity in the State; they saw them take their places at the learned professions, honourably contending with their Protestant countrymen for those prizes and dignities, the rewards of superior scholarship and intellectual attainments; they saw them enriching the literature of their country with their writings, and contributing to the advancement of science and art; they saw them take their seats in the Imperial Parliament, adorning that assembly by their eloquence, their wisdom, and moderation; they saw them occupy the judicial bench, where by their learning and abilities, their entire freedom from prejudice (the first essential in a judge), by their patient and elaborate investigation into the cases brought before them, and their anxiety to establish truth and promote justice,—"Bearing their faculties so meek, and being so clear in their high office," they served as models, such as even Protestants,—ay, and some of them their fellow-judges too, might copy with advantage.

All this was due to the passing of the Emancipation Act,—that act of long-delayed justice, which should have been granted voluntarily, but which was conceded grudgingly, and under a pressure that could no longer have been withstood,—wrung, as it were, from a reluctant king and an unwilling Parliament. And who was this Act, which may be called the Irish Magna Charta, due to? We answer, unhesitatingly, to Daniel O'Connell. He was not only the leader, but the life and soul of the movement that accomplished it—the animating spirit that gave it vitality, strength, and vigour. He it was who infused hope, courage, and confidence into the hearts of his down-trodden, abased, and disheartened countrymen. That he was assisted by able and earnest men of his own creed,—and, to their honour be it mentioned, by eminent liberal-minded Protestants also, both in England and Ireland,—is no doubt true; but his was the guiding hand that organized and directed the whole. Like the champions of old whom we read of, he not only commanded his forces in person, but, fighting single-handed amongst them, and performing prodigies of valour, he inspired them with confidence in him and themselves, and at the same time spread disorder and dismay amongst his foes. Able coadjutors, as we have stated, he no doubt had,—men of learning and talent,—caustic writers, and able speakers; but, without casting a slight upon any of them, we have no hesitation in asserting that the best amongst them was scarcely fit to rank as his lieutenant. Not one of them could have taken his place had he fallen. No general who has ever led his army through dangers and difficulties to ultimate victory, conferring freedom and greatness upon his country, deserves more credit for his services than he did. His task was a herculean one; for he had to contend against the whole weight of English Protestantism, and the concentrated virulence of Irish Toryism, formed as it was into a solid phalanx, and led by men of surpassing talent. With a comparatively feeble press to encourage him, he had to contend against the whole Protestant press of England, Scotland, and Ireland, conducted as it was by men of the greatest learning and ability—practised writers, skilful reasoners, keen logicians. He had to combat against slander, contumely, and contempt—to contend as well against the honest and conscientious political opponent, as against the knave and trickster, who for his nefarious ends wilfully misrepresents motives and actions, so that his best intentions were often misconstrued or distorted. Yet he never lost heart, nor allowed his followers to despair. Gifted with versatile powers, that few other men have ever possessed, with indomitable courage, and untiring energy, he was able at all times to meet his assailants with every weapon they employed against him, and to prove himself a master at the use of each. With the tongue or the pen he was equally ready. Woe to him who entered into paper warfare with him, if his cause was not defensible, and his ability to defend it proven; and woe also to him who entered the lists with him in a war of words! His sarcasms cut to the bone, or fell with blighting force on his adversary, at once reducing him to silence and insignificance. His invectives flew from him with a rapidity and force that crushed and terrified his opponents. When he chose to be satirical, he could scorch and wither, or bring down upon his adversary the laughter and ridicule even of his own supporters. His lofty flights of eloquence charmed and electrified his hearers with their beauty, their originality, and sublimity. He could be grave, severe, didactic, facetious, pathetic, ironical, or declamatory, just as exigency required. Other men have proved themselves great forensic, parliamentary, or political orators; O'Connell was a masterly orator on all subjects. And so he bravely fought his way, undeterred by impediment, dashing every obstacle aside, and deriving renewed courage from their contact, striding confidently towards his desired goal, like a giant exulting in his strength, until, like another Joshua, he led his people out of bondage into the promised land of freedom, divested of their chains, and freed for ever from the disabilities that oppressed them. His victory was culminated by his own entry into the Imperial Parliament as one of the representatives of the people, where now the detractors of this "demagogue," this "mob leader," this "fiery bigot," this "professional agitator," as they used to call him—ay, the very men who so denounced him—in rapt attention and enforced delight were constrained to listen to his matchless eloquence. Well might it have been said of him, that

> "With more than mortal powers endowed,
> How high he soared above the crowd!
> His was no common party race,
> Jostling by dark intrigues for place."

All O'Connell ever sought for was the welfare of his country, and the freedom of his countrymen. All he ever *gained* for his services, which no rewards could adequately repay, was the gratitude of those countrymen. Other men who have performed great services for their country have been rewarded, and justly so, by grants of public money, which have enabled them and their posterity to live in ease and opulence; but this man, who conferred freedom on a nation—who struck from five millions of people fetters the most galling that the slave has ever groaned under, because they not only cut into the flesh, but bound their souls,—this man, who, if he had been actuated by mercenary motives, or by the desire of self-aggrandizement, might have been a modern Crœsus, or attained to high office in the State, died all but penniless! If there were wanting anything to attest his self-abnegation and disinterested character, this fact supplies it. Yes, the great O'Connell died a poor man! That fact alone should enshrine his memory in the heart of every one who values patriotism, honour, and worth.

Let not, therefore, slander with its poisonous breath attempt to sully his memory, or tarnish the lustre of his fame. Let not malice with its envenomed sting distort the motives, or misrepresent the character of the illustrious dead; nor prejudice with its jaundiced eye deny his worth, or detract from his greatness. Let us, now that his ashes sleep in peace amongst us, and nothing but his memory remains, do justice to the man. Let us own the fact, nor be ashamed to do so, that he was a true and genuine patriot—a high and liberal-minded man, and incomparably the greatest Irishman that the past century has produced.

O'Connell has been misrepresented as a narrow-minded

bigot, who availed himself of Protestant support the better to enable him to crush down Protestantism when opportunity offered. No charge more false or unjust has ever been advanced. He had less of true bigotry in his nature than perhaps any man living. Sincerely attached to the form of Christianity he had been born and reared in, but without a particle of what is generally known as Ultramontanism, he only strove for what Protestants would not have less vigorously contended for if placed in similar circumstances—the free liberty of worship for himself and his co-religionists, and the removal of all civil disabilities from those whose religion differed from that established by the State. This he fought for earnestly and manfully; and, in obtaining it, he conferred equal benefit on the Protestant Dissenter as on the Catholic. Some of his most intimate friends were sincere Protestants, and all of them have borne testimony to his genuine liberality in religious matters as well as in political ones. Again, he has been represented as a revolutionist, whose whole object was to separate Ireland from England, and render his country a separate and independent kingdom. All this is false, and without foundation; O'Connell was too wise a man to indulge in such Utopian dreams. No man knew better than he that such a scheme was impracticable. No one valued more highly than he did the connexion of England with this country. No man estimated more highly the noble, the great, the generous English nation—the independence, the liberality, and the indomitable courage of its people. He never dreamt of erecting Ireland into a separate kingdom; what he sought for was to make Ireland the whole sister, and not the step-sister of England,—knowing what a splendid country Ireland was, so rich in natural resources, and so capable of being rendered wealthy and prosperous. Knowing all this, yet seeing his country impoverished and wretched; its resources undeveloped and neglected; its people dragging out a miserable existence for want of industrial employment; the rental of the country—which may be called its life-blood—drawn away to be spent abroad by absentees, instead of returning again to vivify and nourish the source from whence it sprung—seeing, we say, all this, and knowing also the difficulty there was at the time to procure the passing of ameliorative measures for Ireland through the Imperial Parliament, we can well conceive how a man like him should fasten upon the repeal of the legislative union between the two countries, and the establishment in Ireland of a domestic Parliament, as the true panacea for his country's prostrate condition. And stupendous as was the task he undertook, we can well imagine how he, who had carried Emancipation, should not consider its accomplishment impossible. In striving for it he may not, with the cool judgment and calm consideration that mediocre talent summons to its aid, have calculated all the difficulties to be surmounted. His advocacy of the measure may have been a mistake, but other great men have made mistakes too. The first Napoleon—the greatest genius that modern times has produced—made a mistake in leading his mighty army through the steppes of Russia. O'Connell may have erred in his agitation for Repeal; but, if he did, his mistake was a bloodless one. He ever sincerely advocated loyalty to the Throne, and obedience to the laws; and we think his worst detractors must admit that the means he employed for the attainment of his object, while they were the best calculated to effect it, were the least injurious to his country or the empire.

Leaving our hero, David Elliott, and his lovely wife, to pursue the even tenor of their way, we proceed to notice the remaining characters whom we have introduced to the reader. After the defection of our hero from the Grand Lodge of the Purple Arch and the Scarlet Banner, our old acquaintance Bob Coates continued for some time to attend the Lodge as usual, but it was remarked that he did not display the same spirit as formerly, but rather became silent and mopish, continuing, however, to indulge in King Billy's cordial in even more excessive quantities than formerly. At length his constitution, unable to withstand these frightful demands upon his loyalty, gave way, and poor old Bob Coates was attacked with brain fever. For many weeks he battled with this terrible malady, but ultimately, owing to his naturally vigorous constitution, recovered. When he became strong, and able to go about as usual, his brother-Orangemen hovered round him, and induced him to return to his old haunts; for the Grand Lodge of the Purple Arch and the Scarlet Banner had been sadly depleted of late of its most prominent members, so that they could not afford now to lose even one. For a few weeks Bob Coates, true blue to the last, continued to attend as usual to the Lodge; but now his finances, which, like his constitution, had been for a long time in a tottering condition, began to give way, and he became dilatory in his subscription to the funds of the Society, which, owing to their enormous consumption of "rale Protestant punch," required constant replenishing. Finding this to be the case, they at first gave Bob the "cold shoulder;" but as his irregularity increased, and his inability to pay became manifest, his brethren—they who so often treated him to "heart, pocket, and hand"—who knew so well his tried and unshaken loyalty—cut him direct. Bob was disgusted, and cut them in return. Mortified and enraged at his treatment, he sought counsel of his kinsman David Elliott, who, having learned the true state of affairs, like a kind friend as he ever proved, advanced Bob sufficient funds to extricate him from his pecuniary difficulties; and on Coates promising to reform his life, and eschew his intemperate habits, he gave him employment in his establishment, where, thanks to his own industry and to his friend's liberality, he was able to earn a comfortable livelihood. And now Bob Coates commenced to lead a new life; instead of wasting his time in bed, to sleep off the remains of the preceding night's debauch, he rises with the lark, and is a constant attender of the house of God, to which he had for years before been an alien. Instead of despising and hating his Roman Catholic neighbours, he has learned to respect and esteem them. Industrious, moral, religious, he has become in every respect an altered man. And oh, how wondrous was the change thus wrought in old Mr. Coates! When we first presented him to the reader, he only wore the semblance of a man; his whole character was written in his countenance, and the mark of the beast was upon it; for it is a penalty exacted from the drunkard, that his features bear the impress of his life, and unerringly disclose the character of the man. It is as if Moloch, upon whose altar he immolates himself, places his brand upon him; so that all shall know that the demon of drink has laid hold of him, and that the god which he worships is—the bottle! And so it was with poor old Coates; every lineament betrayed the drunkard and the sot. His bleared and bloodshot eyes, inane and expressionless; his unwholesome colour, and his swollen face; his livid lips, and that debased expression of countenance proceeding from the consciousness that he is despised by all men, but by none so heartily as himself,—all proclaimed him the slave of the bottle—the debauchee, and the sot! Such was Robert Coates once; behold him now reformed; for the leper has been cleansed, and the evil spirit has departed from him. The whole aspect of the man is changed; vigour, and even youth, seem to have been imparted to him. His clear and sentient eye reflects the intelligence of a soul within. His face has lost its old besotted look, and bears the stamp of humanity upon it; and now he is no longer ashamed to encounter the gaze of his fellow-man; for he feels that he too is a man, and looks like one. Pleasant and refreshing it is to know that such a change has taken place in him.

As for Deborah, his daughter, fortune favoured her even more than her father. Shortly after Alderman Elliott's marriage, one of the brethren, who had been invited to the wedding dinner we have recorded, and who afterwards had an opportunity of cultivating the young lady's acquaintance at the entertainment that followed, having become smitten with her charms, proposed, and was accepted. This young man, whose name was Doherty, and whom we shall afterwards have occasion to refer to, had been always a favourite with our hero; although a constant attendant at the Lodge, he rarely indulged to excess in drink, and was a remarkably quiet, moral young man. So pleased was Mr. Elliott with the match that had been made, that he set them both up in the "Sign of the Distaff;" for immediately on her marriage his wife retired from that establishment. Deborah, who was a remarkably clever young woman, made herself quite at home in "the Distaff," and did a thriving business. Her husband, who was a most industrious young fellow, also aided her in the management of the establishment; but she was the abler of the two. Old Bob Coates used to stroll up to them in the evenings; and often used he to reflect on his past life, when looking at his son-in-law and his daughter behind their counter, actively plying their customers. "This is the house," he would say, "which belonged to old Nick Lonergan, the man I used to denounce as everything bad and infamous; how unjust and untrue were these charges! Here has my daughter and her husband—the one an Orangeman's daughter, the other an Orangeman himself—been handed over the establishment by the widow of that same Nick Lonergan; they are flourishing in it; and she is only glad they are so. Oh! if I had my life to begin again, I should not be the shallow-minded bigot I have been."

As we have already mentioned, it became the darling object of David Elliott's life to soften down political and religious asperities, and endeavour to create harmonious action between his countrymen, for the good of themselves and their country. With this view, he always made it a point to invite to his house people of different political and religious views, so that, by intermixing with each other, they would gradually lose their prejudices, and learn to respect and bear with each other. And thus it was that the Rev. Boanerges Whackimwell and Father O'Flynn soon became excellent friends. Instead of seeing only the imperfections of each other's character, as was formerly their custom, they learned to lose sight of them, and only to become mindful of the undoubted excellence that each possessed. The consequence was, that Mr. Whackimwell modified the extreme opinions he used to entertain regarding Popery and Popish priests. In Dr. O'Flynn he saw a conscientious, honest, earnest man, labouring faithfully and sincerely to extend and propagate the sacred truths of Christianity by the means, and according to the views, he believed the best and truest. Though differing from him in both, he gave him credit for honesty, sincerity, and zeal. He now looks upon his friend Dr. O'Flynn, not as an emissary of Satan, as formerly, but as his brother-clergyman —his fellow-labourer in the sacred task of spreading and maintaining Christianity through the world. Instead now of striving to make ravages on the flocks of others, while neglecting his own, his first anxiety is to attend to the culture of the fold committed to his care; and now his great learning and talents have an ample field for their exercise. His whole desire now is to promote piety and virtue, peace and love and harmony amongst his people. Instead of the flippant crowd that used to congregate from all parts of the city to hear his wondrous controversial sermons, full of smart sayings and witticisms, and to see religion made the subject of laughter, and the pulpit desecrated with satire and jest, another class assembles, to hear the same man with ability and meekness expound the great truths of the Gospel in language that reaches their heart; for now we can say of Mr. Whackimwell, as Goldsmith says of the "village preacher,"

> "At church, with meek and unaffected grace,
> His looks adorned the venerable place;
> Truth from his lips prevailed with double sway;
> And fools, who came to scoff, remained to pray."

Not greater was the change effected in Dr. O'Flynn: he, too, was fond of indulging in controversy, and of holding up to ridicule the clergymen of the Protestant communion, and the doctrines they professed; but now, like his friend Mr. Whackimwell, he has learned wisdom and moderation, and is not afraid to own the fact. Mixing and conversing with his Protestant neighbours, as he now constantly did, he saw that the religious views both of Protestant and Catholic were in the main almost identical; and that it was unjust and untrue to represent Protestants, as he used to do, as obstinate unbelievers in Christian truth. Hitherto, though he used to proclaim himself a Liberal, his liberalism consisted only in exacting liberality from others, but conceding nothing in return; he has now learned to become liberal himself, which his altered conduct and character plainly evidenced. When a young clergyman of his own communion was once heard, with more zeal than wisdom, to denounce Protestants as a reprobate people, shut out from grace, and a prey to the wiles of Satan, and that there was no approach to heaven save through the portals of the Roman Catholic Church, Dr. O'Flynn rebuked the young man sharply, telling him it lay not with any Church or Churchmen to separate mankind from God; that such doctrine as his young friend had broached savoured only of clerical empiricism, and that to hold it was to insult the majesty of God, and deny his Providence; that God governed not his people by deputy, nor doled out his grace by proxy; that there were other avenues to his mercy than the Church he belonged to; and that all men were Christians who followed the Christian's code, even though they did not construe each clause and section of that code alike—just as lawyers will disagree upon different points of law, and yet remain good lawyers still. He and Dr. O'Flynn, while still sincere and faithful ministers of their respective Churches, became firm friends; and a sort of generous rivalry sprang up between them as to who should exceed the other in their efforts to do good, and as to which of their flocks should excel the other in the observance of every Christian virtue. With truth now might it be said of Dr. O'Flynn, earnest, humble, and pious as he was, as Chaucer wrote of the "Good Parson" more than four hundred years before—

> "A true good man there was there of religion,
> Pious and poor—the parson of a town:
> But rich he was in holy thought and work;
> And thereto a right-learned man; a clerk
> That Christ's pure Gospel sincerely preached,
> And his parishioners devoutly teached.
> Benign he was, and wondrous diligent,
> And in adversity full patient,
>
> . . . .
>
> The lore of Christ and his Apostles twelve
> He taught; but first of all he followed it himselve."

CHAPTER XII.

"Like the leaves of the forest when summer is green,
That host with their banners at sunset were seen;
Like the leaves of the forest when autumn hath blown,
That host on the morrow lay wither'd and strown;
For the angel of death spread his wings on the blast,
And breathed on the face of the foe as he passed;
And the eye of the sleepers waxed deadly and chill,
And their hearts but once heaved, and for ever grew still."

THE withdrawal of Alderman Elliott from the Orange Society proved more disastrous, not only to the section of it with which he was immediately connected, but to the cause generally, than his former associates had anticipated. Shortly after his defection, Sir Toby Jenkins, Sheriff Flooker, and several other leading Orangemen who have not been introduced to the reader, having discussed matters with our hero, also withdrew; and now disorder and dismay possessed the brethren; for the Orange confederation was threatened with disruption. Many of the members, having joined the Association more at the solicitation of friends, or because their ancestors had been previously connected with it, than from principle, continued to support the movement so long as the men they respected, and in whose opinions they had confidence, adhered to it; when, however, these parties had retired, they began to inquire into the reasons that had induced them to do so. These reasons they had no difficulty in ascertaining; for the men who had seceded took care, in their own defence, to give them publicity. The consequence was, that such an exodus from the Orange ranks took place as threatened to eradicate Orangeism altogether from Dublin; in fact, it ultimately was the means of effecting a partial break up of the system; for a sort of interregnum occurred, that lasted for several years, during which Orangeism remained in abeyance, while its fanatical adherents pined and fretted in secret at the decay and breakdown of their beloved institution. These vicious and interested men, however—these stormy petrels of faction—having been unceasing in their efforts to revive the system,—ultimately succeeded in reinstating King Orange on his throne.

As for "the Grand Lodge of the Purple Arch and the Scarlet Banner," in consequence of the defection of its leading man, Alderman Elliott, and of others who had followed his example, it became so depleted of members, that its roll, instead of numbering over one hundred, as it formerly did, was reduced to less than fifty, and of these little more than a dozen regularly attended its meetings. The head of the Lodge now was Con Crawley, who as chairman became so inflated with his imagined importance, that he strutted about with the airs of a man who considered himself one of the props and pillars of the State. The remaining members, with a few exceptions, were men of the same calibre, who, knowing Crawley to be a man of considerable wealth, fawned upon him, and paid him so much deference in consequence, as led the poor old fool to look upon himself as a man of such importance, that without him the business of the Empire could not be proceeded with. One of the persons whom we have excepted, as not forming the same class of men as the older members of the Lodge, was the young fellow named Doherty, who had married Bob Coates's daughter; an earnest, well-meaning man; he had joined the Lodge from a sense of duty, believing it to consist of a combination of high-minded, religious men, banded together for the sacred purpose of maintaining the reformed religion, and combating the assaults of its enemies. There were a few more young fellows who, for similar reasons, retained their names on the roll; but the actual working members were reduced to eight or ten. These men continued to meet as in the palmiest days of the Lodge's prosperity, and to go through the old routine,—indulging each evening in "resolutions," songs, and toasts, and imbibing "rale Protestant punch," in even more inordinate quantities than formerly; for the wretched men sought in the excitement of drink to banish from their minds the melancholy fact, that "the Grand Lodge of the Purple Arch and the Scarlet Banner" was in its declension and decay. Things could not go on for ever thus; the Lodge was receiving no accessions to its members; and unless new blood were infused into it, the body must die of inanition. Con Crawley and his associates now set to work to recruit their diminished ranks at any cost, and by whatever expedient; for such violent fanatics were they, and so unscrupulous in the use of means for the attainment of what they considered was a sacred end, that they determined to leave no effort untried to accomplish their object. At first they endeavoured to obtain volunteers from the members of the various Orange Lodges of Dublin; but, owing to the fact of "the Grand Lodge of the Purple Arch and the Scarlet Banner" having lost its old prestige, and to the fact also of most of the other Lodges being in the same depleted condition, they were unsuccessful in that quarter. They now tried to gain recruits from Protestants generally; but here again they met with failure—for the Orange cause had sunk so low in the estimation of the Protestant community, that they could not induce any one to join them. Baffled thus in their efforts to increase their forces, they resorted to another expedient which proved successful. Finding they could not prevail on grown men to join them, they lay in wait for young lads fresh from the country—medical students, drapers' apprentices, merchants' clerks, and such like, for entrapping whom they displayed the utmost ingenuity. Old settled men, holding for the most part respectable positions in the city, as Crawley and his confederates were, had no difficulty in persuading unsophisticated youths like these to join them, so that they were able to obtain recruits of the kind to any amount.

Once more we find the Lodge restored to its pristine

strength; but that strength was factitious, not real—for, although numerically it stood as formerly, the men composing it were very different from those who had belonged to it in its palmy days. In fact, although the veteran Orangemen had been successful in recruiting their ranks, they had, by the means they resorted to for the purpose, defeated the very ends they had in view. January and May had now met together; and frost and sunshine have never yet agreed. The young men who had joined the Lodge, being for the most part morally and intellectually inclined, had no appetite for drink, nor any desire for indulging in abuse of their Roman Catholic neighbours, many of whom they counted amongst their intimate friends. These young fellows were induced to enrol themselves entirely from conscientious motives, believing that in doing so they were to a certain extent asserting the religious principles they had been reared in. When, however, they found that the sole object for which they assembled in the evenings was to indulge in whiskey punch, and in senseless abuse and ridicule of the Catholics, and of the religious creed they conscientiously entertained, they began to feel that they had been duped and deceived. Having no sympathy with the ignorant and besotted drunkards forming the older members of the Lodge, they separated from them, and formed themselves into a distinct group, animated by entirely different tastes and feelings. An awkward state of things was now presented: here were ten or twelve filthy old drunkards, and some twenty intelligent young fellows, despising drink, and only seeking for innocent and harmless amusement, meeting together, night after night, almost without a feeling in common to bind them together. The consequences were, that the old members stuck to their "loyalty" and their punch, which, with the view of keeping up their spirits, they continued to drink in greater excess than before; while the youthful members amused themselves as they best could. Amongst the latter was a lad named O'Flaherty, who became a general favourite. Tim O'Flaherty played the violin with great skill, sung an excellent song, and was a most entertaining young fellow. When Tim's musical talents were discovered, his companions determined to avail themselves of them, for without some amusement their time used to pass very drearily. After a great deal of opposition on the part of the older members, principally, however, from Crawley, O'Flaherty obtained permission to introduce his violin, by way of serving as an accompaniment to the Orange songs the old fellows were accustomed to bellow forth each night. These songs were of the most violent and abusive character, each having generally a chorus, in which all the members present were expected to join. At first, true to the understanding entered into, O'Flaherty confined himself to playing accompaniments of the kind; but his companions, tired of the continual reiteration of them, insisted on his playing something new. And now, despite the remonstrances of Con Crawley and his confreres, the sprightly tones of "The Wind that shakes the Barley," "Garryowen," "The Rakes of Mallow," "Sir

Roger De Coverley," and such like airs, might be heard within the sanctified walls of the Lodge; while the younger brethren, animated by their inspiriting strains, would get up and dance, one portion personating ladies. Thus they would get through a jig, a reel, or a quadrille—a dance just then becoming fashionable; the non-performing portion of their companions, in convulsions of laughter, looking on applaudingly; while the old fellows, who despised and abhorred such enormities, would throw down bumper after bumper of "King Billy's cordial" to smother their rage, gnashing their teeth in impotent fury at the desecration thus perpetrated. Bitterly did they now repent of having introduced into their ranks the younger members; but their regrets came too late—they were but a handful as compared to their juniors, whose numbers as regards the old stagers were as three to one.

Our brilliant countryman, Thomas Moore, was just now publishing his beautiful "Irish Melodies," which will live so long as language endures; and Tim O'Flaherty, having a rich and powerful voice, used to sing them with a taste and feeling that thrilled to the hearts of all who heard him. Terrible was the scene that took place when O'Flaherty, on the solicitation of his comrades, first sang within the hallowed walls "Dear Harp of my Country." Oh, how stale and flat now appeared the stupid Orange songs they were accustomed to hear yelled out by Con Crawley, or bellowed forth by the husky voices of his besotted companions.

The break-up of "the Grand Lodge of the Purple Arch

and the Scarlet Banner" may be dated from the occasion when Tim first sang this melody: for, once having heard it, his associates refused to listen to any of the Orange songs they used formerly submit to. Whenever any of the old stagers would venture upon one of them, he was coughed down by his young associates, or reduced to silence by Timothy's violin; for, loud as they would roar out their favourite chorus of

"Lero, lero, lillibulero;
Lillibulero, bullen a la;
Lillibulero, lillibulero, lillibulero, bullen a la,"

that young fellow, with some inspiriting lively air, would dash in and drown their voices. An open rupture now occurred between the old and the new members: the former, though a small minority, insisted in right of their long connexion with the Lodge on carrying out their views; but the latter, because of their numbers, insisted that they were entitled to enforce theirs. Every night now a scene of riot and disorder was enacted. The Lodge had become completely disorganized, and could no longer be designated an Orange Lodge at all: for the only remnant of "loyalty" that used to be indulged in was "King Billy's cordial," the use of which was almost exclusively confined to the older members, who amply made up by their frightful excesses for the abstinence of their juniors. Some of the more wild and thoughtless of the young fellows, to break the monotony of the evening, would now sally out and attack the "watch," and afterwards return with their spoils, consisting of the lanterns, poles, and rattles of the unfortunate "Charlies;" these they would deposit in triumph on the table amid the cheers and applause of their companions, but beneath the indignant scowls of Con Crawley and his associates. In such wild freaks young Doherty never participated. From his connexion with Alderman Elliott he used frequently to meet that gentleman and his son, who omitted no opportunity of dissuading him from continuing an Orangeman; and the young man was at length beginning to see the vicious and useless nature of the system.

The other members of the Lodge now proceeded from one excess to another. Having altogether ceased to acknowledge the authority of the chairman, whom they frequently threatened to displace, they acted just as they pleased, setting their elder brethren completely at defiance. Many of them having amongst their acquaintances several Roman Catholic friends, used to introduce them night after night to the *sanctum sanctorum* of the Lodge, contrary to the rule of the Society. Some of these young fellows had excellent voices, and now formal concerts began to be held night after night; and, instead of the violent party songs with which the walls of the Lodge used to resound, duets and glees, having no political nor sectarian character, admirably sung, accompanied as usual by Tim O'Flaherty on the violin, were constantly heard. Against all this the elder members of the Lodge loudly protested, indignantly denouncing all who took part in such unhallowed innovations as revolutionists and rebels. At length it happened one evening, when Crawley and his confreres had given more than ordinary opposition to the amusement indulged in by the young men, and had denounced them with more than usual acerbity, that Tim O'Flaherty, from love of mischief, and to spite the elder members for their disagreeable conduct, sang "Oh, breathe not his name," that beautiful and pathetic melody which Thomas Moore has composed on the memory of our gifted countryman, Robert Emmett, whose sad fate was within the recollection of most of his hearers. During the delivery of it, the old men, stunned at the cool audacity of O'Flaherty, and absolutely palsied with horror and amazement, sat motionless; but when Timothy had ended, Con Crawley, livid with rage, and frothing at the mouth with fury, rose from his seat, and, throwing a look of concentrated hate at O'Flaherty and his friends that rendered him for the moment frightful to look upon, exclaimed with an excitement and wildness of manner partaking of frenzy—

"Have we got amongst haythens or man-eaters? Am I Cornelius Crawley the loyalist, or Felix O'Flanagan the Ribbonman and rebel? Am I in a hideous drame?—and are those I see before me demons, and not men? I mind the time when, if any mimber dare to utter a disloyal word in this room, 'tis out of that windy he'd be dropped on the pavement. I remimber when every one attending this Lodge was so loyal that, even when overcome with liquor, and unable to keep his legs, he was able to cry out 'Croppy, lie down.' I mind the time when the wakest individual amongst us could swallow his one-and-twenty tumblers of the best of rale Protestant punch, and many of us on a stretch could make his three dozen, carrying it all discreetly home like Christians, and still being able to give utterance to the same loyal sintiment. But how do we stand now? Here's 'the Grand Lodge of the Purple Arch and the Scarlet Banner,' that has disposed of whole puncheons of the best 'parliament,' and has levelled so many anathemas on the head of the Pope, that in all fairity that ould man and his followers ought long ago to be sunk at the bottom of the say. Here is that once noble Lodge composed of what?—why, with the exception of myself, and my loyal followers around me, of a set of cockatrices, deceptioners, and traitors, under cover, my dear, of Protestants,—a collection of mane, unmanly fellows, who haven't the sperit to swallow a drop of drink, nor the courage to scrame out 'No surrender!' or 'Down with the Pope!'"

"Who's a traitor, Crawley?" asked young Doherty, stepping forward, in great excitement; while his companions waited with breathless impatience to see the termination of the scene.

Crawley, who was excited also, and much the worse for liquor, replied—

"You are one of them: for, despite of all your pretended loyalty, you've gone over to the enemy. Confusion seize the whole pack of you! Yez all are traitors!"

"What, Crawley! am I one?" asked O'Flaherty, with indignation in his countenance.

Regarding his questioner with a look in which the concentrated hate of a thousand demons was depicted, Crawley replied—

"Get out, you bad mimber! You are not only a

traitor, but a rebel! You're a spy, an informer, and an emissary of Popery! I hate you! I spit upon you! We have had neither luck nor grace since you and your infernal 'Cremona,' as you call it, came amongst us. You're not a Protestant, but a blackguard! You're a Papist!—a Jesuit in disguise!—and if I thought you could be anything worse nor that, I'd say it!"

"I tell you what it is, Crawley!" exclaimed Doherty, "that the humblest and most ignorant Papist that ever crawled on his bare knees for penance, believing that in doing so he was pleasing God, is superior to you: for he is animated by a devotional feeling which has never actuated you. It is you who are no Protestant. You foul and filthy old man, you are a disgrace to humanity! You are no more deserving of the name of Protestant than the sow that wallows in the mire! I am happy to own that I have many Roman Catholic friends, who are all both morally and religiously as superior to you, as anything that is honest and good is to that which is base and vile!"

For some moments Crawley could not realize the fact that he had really been thus assailed by Doherty; for that young man had been hitherto most quiet and subservient to him and his companions. When, however, he had recovered himself, and become aware of the actual truth, he turned upon the youth who had thus braved him, and in a voice of thunder exclaimed—

"How dare you, you worm, address me thus? How have you the audacity, you nobody, to speak to me so!—to me who, with the gallant few around me, have for years upheld Protestantism against all assailants?"

Here Tim O'Flaherty burst into an uproarious fit of laughter that drowned every other voice.

"What's the fun, Tim?" asked several of his companions, not seeing anything in what had occurred to provoke such merriment.

"The idea"—exclaimed O'Flaherty, attempting an explanation, but, unable to proceed, breaking again into uproarious laughter, which actually obliged him to press his hands to his sides, as if to keep himself from bursting.

"Well, what idea?" asked his companions, growing impatient. "Come, let's have it."

"The idea," said O'Flaherty, at length finding utterance, "of the Protestant religion being upheld by such a jolly old humbug as Con Crawley!" And the young fellow again indulged in roars of laughter, in which all his companions, struck with the absurdity of the notion, heartily joined. When the merriment had subsided, one of the young men exclaimed—

"Not only is Crawley a humbug, but Orangeism is a humbug also!"

"It's a fraud upon the public, and a burlesque upon Protestantism!" cried another.

"It is a combination of drunkards, dupes, and hypocrites!" exclaimed a third.

"I tell you what Orangeism is," said Doherty—"it is worse than what any of you have characterized it. It is Protestant Ribbonism, that's what it is—yes, Protestant Ribbonism—differing from the Romish system in this, that the members of the one are ignorant, unlettered peasants, having grievances to complain of; while the Orange Ribbonman is comparatively educated, and has no grievances at all. The one has some pretext for his conduct, the other has none."

"Let us dissolve, then," cried several voices. "The whole affair is a humbug."

"And Con Crawley," exclaimed O'Flaherty, "is the king of humbugs!"

"Crown him!" cried one of the young fellows.

Immediately upon this, one of his companions, seized the capacious punch jug, that stood partially filled on the table, and pressed it down tightly on Crawley's head, while the contents falling around him, almost blinded the wretched old man by its pungent alcoholic nature.

"There," exclaimed the young man who had done the deed, "I have crowned and anointed him at the same time."

Crawley's friends now gathered round him, eagerly proffering their services to extricate him out of his predicament, while peal upon peal of laughter proceeded from the thoughtless young men. With some difficulty the punch jug was removed from his head, taking with it his wig. And now Crawley presented a frightful appearance. Rage and anger tenfold greater than before possessed him, transforming him for the time into a very fiend. His countenance, usually of a beet-root hue, became a livid white, relieved by a few spots of crimson, imparting to it a hideously sinister expression; while his eyes, inflamed with the drink he had partaken of, and with that which had just entered them, rolled in his head like balls of fire. Recovering himself from the spasm of wrath that at first had seized him, he levelled the most hideous imprecations on O'Flaherty and his associates, displaying, as he did so, a fluency and originality of expression that seemed as if some fiend was at his ear inspiring him, so hideously unique were the anathemas he pronounced.

"As for you, O'Flaherty," said he, as, exhausted with fury, he drew to a close, "again I say, take with you my living, burning, bitter curse,—may it clothe you with leprosy from head to foot; and take with you also the accumulated curse of every Orangeman in Ireland; for I will blast you over the entire country, so that all our voices shall ascend in one consuming malediction that shall bring down ruin, destruction, and death upon you."

When he had ceased, O'Flaherty quietly asked him had he anything more to say, to which Crawley rejoined by spitting like a noisome reptile at him.

To the intense amusement of his companions, Tim replied to this salute, by placing his violin in position and striking up the well-known Irish air bearing the suggestive but somewhat inelegant title of "Go to the devil and shake yourself;" and now, amid roars of laughter, he and his companions divesting themselves of their orange scarves, and, throwing them at Con Crawley and his associates, hurried out of the room, and proceeded up the street, O'Flaherty still playing the same enlivening air.

Crawley's companions now condoled with him for the indignities he had been subjected to. One of them wiped his head and face; another dried his wig, and replaced it on his head; while they all joined with him in denouncing O'Flaherty and his associates, and heaping curses on their heads. Restored to something like composure, the first object of the old fellows was to replenish the punch jug. One of them, who was the landlord of the house, undertook the duty; and soon he returned with the vessel, which contained over three gallons, charged to the brim with the fiery compound. The Orangemen, who were six in number, commenced to drink with a frightful recklessness, Crawley in his excitement swallowing tumbler after tumbler of the scalding, reeking liquid, as if it had been water. Naturally a conceited man, having an overweening opinion of his importance, the shock his vanity had received had stunned him so completely, that, after his first outbreak of wrath was over, he became silent and subdued; but now, having drunk so fearfully, his spirits returned, and rose to an unnatural height. After drinking confusion to the young men who had left, he insisted on toasting each of his companions; he next obliged each to sing an Orange song, the rest all joining in the chorus; and the discordant sounds thus produced, as the drunken old men endeavoured to raise the wild refrain, was actually fearful. A mad excitement seized upon them all; the punch jug was replenished again; and now

Con Crawley, who was in a state of drunken frenzy, proposed that they should drink against each other, in order to see which was the best toper. To this the others assented; but one of them, who retained a little more consciousness than the rest, started the objection that they had no means of ascertaining who would be the victor; "for," said he, "when we all become fuddled, how can we tell who was the last to give in?"

"Come," said Con Crawley, seeing the point made by his companion, "let each of us deposit a guinea upon the table, and he who is the victor will become winner of the stakes; the possession of them will establish his triumph."

The remainder of the brethren concurring in this proposal, they each produced the coin and laid it upon the table; and now they proceeded methodically to work to drink down each other, each of them taking bumper for bumper. Having drunk heavily all the night before, they were not able to continue long at this beastly competition; one by one they gave in,—some of them falling from their seats like senseless logs, others dropping their heads upon the table in beastly stupefaction, and remaining there senseless lumps of animated clay. Only two now retained consciousness, Con Crawley being one, and the landlord of the house, whom we have before referred to, the other; it was now a struggle between the two; and, drunk as both were, they felt the excitement of the contest; again they helped themselves to the fiery compound; Crawley raised his glass to his lips and drained it; his companion attempted to imitate him, but before he could swallow the whole, his head reeled, and, casting on the other an idiotic stare, he dropped from his seat and joined his senseless companions.

"Ah, ha!" screamed Crawley, exultingly, "Ah, ha! I've won!—the stakes are mine!—I've triumphed!" and, throwing one hand forward, he closed upon the six pieces of gold, while with the other he raised the punch ladle to help himself to a further supply of the terrible liquid; but on stooping forward to do so, his breath, gaseous with alcohol, catching the flame of the candle, ignited into a bright blue flame; a convulsive spasm seized him—he choked—his frame quivered for a moment, and was still; for all that now remained of Cornelius Crawley was—dust and ashes. Death was so instantaneous, that he retained the same position he had occupied when his breath had caught fire; there he remained, his chest leaning forward upon the edge of the table, one hand still covering the guineas to secure which he had lost his life, the other still grasping the punch ladle. Meantime the flame continued to burn, darting from his mouth in a continuous jet, which after a time extended to his face, and thence to his body, encompassing him in a pale blue flame, now varying to a greenish tint, then to a light yellow, but always returning to the same light bluish hue that had first appeared. The fact was, that Crawley having for months past drunk inordinately, his whole system had become as it were alcoholized; his blood had assimilated itself to the spirituous fluid, and his flesh and bones had undergone a chemical change, all more or less partaking of the nature of alcohol, so that the remains of the wretched man, as if impregnated with a resinous substance, burnt as freely as charcoal. Hideous and ghastly was the scene now presented: the flame began to shift and vary in its course, at one time completely covering the body in its terrible embrace, causing it to appear one entire mass of fire, at another contracting itself into a comparatively narrow compass; now attacking the head, now the trunk, next the extremities, then again expanding into one blaze, devouring the whole body; thus it continued its consuming course, like a greedy monster, capricious in its appetite, seeking for choice places to batten on, yet still remorselessly intent on devouring the entire; and thus the hideous holocaust went on, a foul yellow vapour ascending from it that curled and twined itself into a hundred fantastic shapes, seeming like so many demons exulting in the horrible burnt sacrifice to the demon of drink. The candles were now extinguished, having burned themselves out, and the room was alone lighted by the unearthly flame, throwing a sinister light around, that caused every object to assume strange fantastic forms; casting its unwholesome glare over the five prostrate drunkards, whose sleep was destined to be that which knows no waking. All through that dreadful night the flames continued their remorseless course, eating and burning up the remains of this wretched man, until, having consumed the whole, they died away from want of fuel; and now all that remained was a mass of calcined bones, a horrid, grinning, blackened skeleton, still retaining the exact position the body held when the spark of life was first quenched. So peculiar was this fire, that, although it grazed and touched the table and the very chair on which the skeleton was seated, it would not burn, but only charred these objects; requiring as it were more inflammable material to exercise its consuming powers on; the feast afforded it was so dainty, it would not waste itself on any other substance. And now morning came, and the domestics of the house arose to perform their daily functions; for it was the custom with these people to retire to rest, leaving their master remaining up with his companions. No sound issued from the chamber of death—nothing escaped from it but a foul and noisome vapour, that was penetrating every corner of the house with its stifling breath. The servants gazed at each other in amazement and terror; the landlord's family were aroused; the door of "the Grand Lodge of the Purple Arch and Scarlet Banner" was burst open; they attempted to enter, but, in doing so, were driven back by the stifling vapour that escaped from the room. One, more bold than the rest, rushed in, and, unclosing the shutters, raised one of the windows; and, oh! terrible was the scene now presented in this "chamber of horrors." There was the charred skeleton of Crawley sitting at the table, as if still animated with life, grinning at them with a hideous leer, like some exultant demon from the depths of the infernal regions, exulting over the scene of desolation and death; the blackened fleshless fingers of one hand still clasping the punch ladle, the calcined fingers of the other still covering the pieces of gold.

There were the five men who had engaged with Crawley in the dreadful competition of drunkenness, in the positions they had occupied when they had each succumbed to the stupefying influence of the deadly liquor they had swallowed, arrayed still in their orange scarves,—all stone dead—stiffened corpses, either smothered in their drink, or poisoned by the noxious gases that were evolved in the fiery process that had taken place. Dismay and horror possessed all who witnessed this dreadful scene. The party emblems through the room seemed to aggravate the surrounding horrors; for, as if in mockery, there was seen high over all, in gilt letters on a purple ground, forming an arch above the chimneypiece—"THE GLORIOUS, PIOUS, AND IMMORTAL MEMORY."

The family of the wretched man who had owned the house, and who had been one of the victims immolated, at once abandoned the premises, which remained shut up for years. Fearful stories were circulated now as to the men who resorted to the establishment, which, by being retailed, became invested with new horrors. It was said that the revellers who had frequented the house had bartered their souls away to the evil one; and that, to enable them the better to endure the torments of perdition when their time came, they used to roast themselves before a burning fire to season themselves to the flames—that at midnight, Satan, finding his followers all ripe for his purposes, ascended and carried them away with him. These, and stories even of a wilder and more improbable nature, began to be circulated. And now the house, which was fast falling to ruins, became an object of terror to all who looked upon it; the ravens nestling in the chimneys used to be set down as the departed spirits of the frequenters of the house, hovering round the scene of their former excesses; people declared that they heard at night the voices of the revellers chorusing to their songs as of yore. The night watchman, as he passed the house, felt a chill of horror creep around him, and avoided its precincts; mothers with their infants in their arms would clasp their burdens more tightly to their bosoms, and pass to the other side of the street in terror. Every one avoided the house as if a curse had fallen upon it. At length, one stormy night in January, the chimneys fell in, carrying the roof and all the floors along with them; and now nothing but the walls remained. Years rolled on, during which the place continued a ruin, until a stranger, unacquainted with its history, obtained a lease of the ground, removed the debris, and built a new house on the site. The horrors connected with the place then became forgotten. Such was the close of "the Grand Lodge of the Purple Arch and the Scarlet Banner."

THE END.

CPSIA information can be obtained
at www.ICGtesting.com
Printed in the USA
LVHW022005120422
716028LV00006B/326

9 783752 595307